I0760652

BEYOND THE RHODODENDRONS

A. B. Snow

BEAR PRESS

ISBN
Hardback: 978-1-999-710224
Softcover: 978-1-999- 710231
eBook: 978-1-999-710248

A CIP record for this book is available
from the British Library

For Bear Press
Development: Lucy York
Editor: Sarah Fish
Art Director: Sarah Joy

Set in 11/15pt PT Serif

1v04

For my own fair Helena

1 – A Late Night Bus Ride

The negligée-clad blonde was making eyes at me. I wasn't paying her the attention she deserved, that is, until she spoke.

"Did you know?" she said. There might have been a few other choice words too, but my mind was scrabbling to catch up with the fact that a photograph in a Bristol bus shelter had just addressed me.

"Pardon?" I said, more to myself, for fear of scaring her off.

The broken neon lights of the advert flickered on and off rhythmically, alternately revealing her beauty and, by turn, my own gaunt visage in the glass—ragged, unkempt beard and somewhat lank light brown hair.

'More forty-eight than twenty-eight,' a morose inner voice said. I call him Mr Cautious, although Mr Gloomy would better suit his demeanour. I ignored him and, regarding the flawless skin in front of me, decided the lips had not, could not have moved.

I could definitely hear something though, and it wasn't in my head.

I looked around; the shelter was empty. I turned off the music and removed my earphones to better listen.

The rain was crying softly into the late darkness—the street abandoned. One voice. Very clear. Angry. No, hurt. I left the shelter to look around the back, and as I did so, she entered at the far end. Her eyes glanced around the now empty space as I froze. She didn't see me. Clearly, she was unhappy.

I judged her to be no older than me. She sobbed "No" and stared at her phone, hitting it with the palm of her hand in frustration before sinking onto the uncomfortable aluminium plank so favoured by city designers.

Perhaps this morning her long dark hair had been straightened and brushed, framing her square face and determined jaw, but now it was askew and beaded with rain. Her eyelashes had run black streaks down her cheeks, her brow was furrowed, and her short tartan skirt and crop-top were too skimpy for the night air, probably decided on when the late spring day had shown its false promise of sun, now long gone.

She was tall, and if the perfume model in the advert was beautiful, then this girl was on the 'handsome' end of the scale. Athletic, definitely, and the word 'tomboy' came to mind. Her pale green eyes peered out from under a black fringe and two dimples accentuated her wide mouth. Her lips were neither thin nor too broad—just perfect lips—currently twisted in a slightly puzzled way which, with her furrowed brow, reminded me for some reason of a pirate. I admired what I saw.

Her boots, worn with socks tucked almost out of view, were robust and functional, at odds with the softness of the outfit, but they added somewhat to the 'distressed punk' vibe. It all seemed a bit out of place. I wondered if it was the look she had been hoping for.

Australian, I thought for a moment, and then realised the words I had overheard had not sounded particularly southern, just strange. She was breathing deeply, very ragged on the exhale, and that might be what affected her speech. Maybe she was in a hurry to catch the bus.

As I watched her take another long breath, it looked more like she had just run very hard, and the audible quavering suggested she had been running from something or someone. I expected to see fear, but instead she looked alert and wary.

No suitcase, no bag of any kind. Surely she would not have come out without a bag? So, she left in a hurry then. Or she's on her way home, like me. Her left knee was freshly grazed. No bag, and a fall.

At work, my analysis was sharp, but this was not a computer, but a human, and the variables were not so easy to decipher. I was puzzled.

I was staring at her knee when I realised she was staring at me. It was too late to look away nonchalantly, as though I had been but glancing in her direction. I was truly caught. I decided to re-enter the shelter. At least, I thought, I hadn't been staring at her chest, and then realised I now was. Hurriedly I looked up. She was tensed, as if she was about to rush at me but thought better of the distance, and instead was trying to play it cool.

"I fell," she said.

"I'm sorry." I tried to excuse myself. "I didn't mean to stare." She was watching me closely, as though she expected me to perform some magician's trick.

"Well it makes a change from looking at my boobs," and I coloured as she laughed. It wasn't a happy laugh, but the corners of her eyes crinkled. I liked that. She was still poised on the edge of the seat, ready to leap. Or maybe run.

Irish, I thought. No, another inner voice supplied—probably Scottish, like those doing the curling on TV.

This had a disastrous impact as my currently unsettled mind grasped at the straw.

"Do you curl?" I asked, and simultaneously died at the lameness of the thought.

The question caught her off guard and we stared at each other. The few seconds allowed her to catch up.

"No," she replied. "I was born in St Andrews, but not all of us play with the 'wee' stones."

The way she emphasised the 'wee' suggesting she was affecting her accent to suit my typecasting. She took the opportunity to lift herself carefully off the seat, so smoothly that I hardly noticed she had risen.

"When does the bus come?" she continued. Her head was slightly to one side, judging, evaluating, sizing me up. I wondered what she wanted.

I had now progressed, in duration, beyond the normal

length of conversation with someone of the opposite species. 'Opposite *sex*,' an inner critic corrected me. I found myself at a loss, therefore, and not sure what should happen next. I had always found myself woefully short in the small-talk department and I was desperate to avoid any more comments about curling. However, I was also still struggling with the complexity of the variables before me, and beginning to wonder if I should leave, quickly. My mind peeled away on an increasingly random curve. I found I was unable to speak.

"The bus?" she repeatedly slowly. "What time does it come?" I could see her shoulders move as she tensed again. I wanted to look behind me for the exit but her agile grace and frankly dangerous demeanour commanded my full attention.

"Ugh." I tried to pull myself together, desperate to fill the silence. I stared again, but in trying to avoid her enquiring eyes, my gaze dropped. This did nothing to help my thought processes—her very presence disturbed my entire being.

She straightened, facing me across the concrete floor, lifting her arms behind her head, arching herself backwards to stretch, backlit by the red LED sign that helpfully told us to 'refer to timetable'.

So carefully had I been watching her hands that I did not notice how close to me she had moved. Now she stood right in front of me, her eyes almost dead level with mine. 'That makes her nearly six foot,' an inner voice supplied. 'A bit less if those boots have any insoles.' I sighed. I called him Mr Logical, but I wished he would devote his energy to the principles of muscle movement, in particular to the running-away muscles in my legs.

"The bus?" This time it sounded like a threat. Close up, I had no chance. I had lost all rational thought. I looked about wildly.

I was saved by the sight of headlights laying down tracks in the wet road, bouncing their way towards us. Incoherent, I merely pointed and her eyes followed, as the Number 9 slowed, and its doors hissed open.

I stood aside, partly to let her on first, but mostly to give myself a chance to think about catching another bus, even though I knew there wasn't one. She passed me, eyes never leaving mine, until she stepped up to the driver's window.

Then I watched as she argued with the driver as to why buses no longer took cash—her shoulders slumped as the fifty-pound note she had pulled from her phone failed to garner the effect she wanted. I was suddenly tired, and cold, and I realised that under the brighter glare of bus light, her height did nothing to hide a very real vulnerability. I sighed, climbed the step, reached out and held my bus card over the metal snout. As it beeped, I waved her towards the seating.

"Thanks," she muttered, glaring once more at the driver, then at me, before she stalked and sat down a few rows back.

I waved my card again, heard the ever-so-happy chirp of a machine making money, and moved towards the back of the bus. I didn't try to catch her eye as I passed. Whatever this was, it probably wasn't about me, and if it was, I was in no state to talk about it.

I sat down in the centre of the back seat, and re-evaluated the evidence. I noticed my usually loquacious internal advisers were silent; the reality of this girl did not match up with any fantasy in which I usually wandered.

I didn't mean to close my eyes, but when I did so I could still see the perfume model's face, flickering in and out of view as the light went on and off. Each time she disappeared, I imagined not my own countenance reflected, but rather the pale menacing scowl rimmed with the dark, wet hair of the girl now sitting ahead of me.

Whether this was fantasy or reality, I decided it was best if it was over.

And it would have been, if I hadn't drifted off.

2 – Safe for the Night

I've heard that romance is dead, but if I believed that then, I don't believe it now. Rather, I think that sometimes she hides shyly, just beyond the rhododendrons of life, and all it takes is one moment, one chance seized—the viewpoint changes—and through the humdrum shrubbery, we glimpse the flower. Perhaps romance is merely the act that allows our viewpoint to change, but as it turned out, I didn't really understand rhododendrons.

"Come on, we're here." Her voice roused me and, disorientated, I assumed I had reached my destination and stumbled for the door. The rain had diminished, replaced by a fog—something I realised as I saw the red tail-lights of the bus evaporate into the gloom.

With the weather update came another thought: I don't live here—this empty country lane certainly wasn't my stop and as far as I could remember wasn't even on the route. I opened my mouth to protest, but a triple conflict left me speechless. Why was I *here*? Why was *she* here, and why was I watching the last bus disappear into the night?

At least the rain had stopped. More or less.

"Come on," she repeated and, crooking her arm through mine, she started walking.

"Where are we going?" I managed.

"To mine. Shhh," she silenced me. My hoodie, though zipped up, wasn't much help against the cold wet air. Her body was pressed into my side, which was both comforting and unsettling.

We turned off the lane into the woods, and as we did so, she shivered. I sighed, stopped, unzipped my hoodie, and gave it to her. Her eyes held mine as she thought for a moment. Then she slid her left arm into the garment, motioned for me to do the same with my right. This brought us even closer to each other, but made walking a little trickier—like a pair of drunken revellers.

Soon I felt gravel underfoot and my eyes, growing accustomed to the dark, made out a path. She seemed familiar with it, but used her phone occasionally to highlight the way. We trudged together for what seemed like forever but was probably only twenty minutes. The woods gave way on the right to a hedge, and she announced:

"Here we are."

Her phone illuminated a blue door outlined by a stone arch nestled in a gap in the hedge. She waved her phone at the right-hand pillar and the gate unlocked.

I followed, or more precisely I was dragged along by the animated half of my hoodie, past the assorted bric-a-brac of a garden. She no longer needed her phone as a torch. The path gave way to cobbles, and out of the gloom I saw the dark outline of a large building with a glazed double door.

She paused, slipping her arm out of our common garment as she did so. There was a thunk, and she almost pushed me through the entrance. I heard her let out a deep sigh as the door closed with another thunk that suggested it would not be opening again any time soon.

She switched on a light, revealing a utilitarian hallway.

"Take off your shoes," she ordered, and I did so, even though the stone floor was unlikely to be marked by them.

"Now come on, hurry up." She led me through a room and up some plain but expensively carpeted stairs. I thought it unlikely that I had been picked up for casual sex, but even so I found myself wondering how soon it would become apparent that whatever I had to offer her, it was not experience.

The passageway widened and we stopped at a large panelled door. She opened it and stood aside.

"In here."

The bedroom seemed to be the size of a small house. Centrally placed against one wall was the grandest bed I had ever seen. On the opposite wall were two cupboards with a small desk between them. The room was warm and the sight of a bed seemed to release my tiredness. I felt overwhelmed by exhaustion.

"Take off your trousers."

"Look," I started, "I think ..."

"Just do it," she said, and I complied, removing the hoodie and damp socks as well. "Now lie down." She pulled back the covers to emphasise her point.

I lay down. She crossed the room to hang up my clothes, rummaged in the cupboard, and, returning, leapt astride me. I could feel her thighs and the damp edges of her skirt pinning me down as she leant forward.

"Now," she continued, "don't read anything into this ..." I had no idea what *this* was, and so I found myself watching with detachment as she wrapped a handcuff around my left wrist, and then attached the other end to the bedstead.

"You're sleeping in here." She swung herself up and off the bed, and looked down at me. She pulled up the covers and suddenly I went from being someone who was hoping against the odds to explore a bit more of a girl than I ever had explored before, to being a small boy tucked in by his mother. I had a year of psychology before I'd dropped out, but I'm not sure we had covered this.

"You see, I only know three things about you." She counted them off on her fingers: "One, I think you like to escape from things, like from reality, right?" I could only manage a small nod.

"Two, you notice things. Not just my boobs, but my phone, my shoes, no bag, my knee, the shivering."

I just looked at her as she bent to smooth the sheet and blanket over me.

"And three, you were kind enough to pay my bus fare and then not expect to chat me up afterwards."

Well, I thought to myself, at least this last item seemed an unlikely prelude to grievous bodily harm, and so I relaxed a little.

"So, here we are," she continued. "Maybe you've 'pulled', as they say in the movies. But right now I have a problem and I don't want you ... attacking me in my bed as I sleep. So be a good boy, and I'll see you in the morning."

She walked to the door, turned off the light and shut the door behind her.

As I lay in the dark, I realised three things myself. One, I was not convinced by her 'attack me in my bed' speech—it had sounded more like she had started to say she didn't want me 'running off'.

Two, the chain on the cuffs was longer than I had initially thought and I could get out of bed, and even switch on the bedside light. A light green towel was folded at the foot of the sturdily made frame. I glanced at my trousers which she had folded neatly on the stand across the room, with my own phone in my pocket, so near, yet so far.

As I towelled off my damp hair, the third, and by far most disturbing, discovery was that I was not particularly worried by the events I had just experienced. I could feel my heart beating exultantly inside my chest, and I thought that this excitement was because my world-as-I-knew-it had shifted, and that there was now a glimpse of a gap through the metaphorical shrubbery—a gap I was keen to explore.

I didn't know what the 'problem' was that she had mentioned, but right now I had a bed that wouldn't fit into my garage flat, and soft sheets that almost purred as I sank back into them. Somewhere, close by, was a girl, who may or may not be psychotic, but who seemed to have some very definite ideas about sex.

As I drifted off to sleep, I heard Mr Grumpy, long-time colleague to Mr Logical, rightfully point out that she had only said 'maybe you've pulled', but I considered that even if she didn't like me, she at least didn't completely dislike me.

I slept.

3 – Rudimentary Ablutions

Monday morning dawned. I awoke to the clink of cups and fond memories of home, but as I propped myself up, the steel around my wrist reminded me of where I was and how I had come to be here. I blinked at the vest-clad girl standing over me.

"Helena Fey," she said, head slightly to one side, as she set down the tray and handed me a mug. The tea was sturdy looking. One had to appreciate a girl who could make a cup of tea that looked like that. 'Or who locked you up'—Mr Logical was now also awake, or maybe it was his sidekick, Mr Cautious.

She looked different. I took a small sip of tea, to give myself time to think. As far as I could reconstruct last night, none of it made much sense.

She crossed the room and pulled the cord to open the curtains. Silhouetted against the early light, she walked back towards me, her eyes fixed on mine. She rounded and then sat down on the edge of the bed without breaking her gaze. I wondered if I could escape, but suddenly there were more pressing problems.

"I need to go to the bathroom." I also wondered if this would be a good time to escape.

"I'm sorry," she said, "how rude." She leant over me to unfasten the cuff about my wrist, the key disappearing back into her joggers. She pointed to a door behind me.

The room was only slightly smaller than the bedroom, a very temple of ablution. Clearly the architect had not been looking to achieve a compact arrangement. I had a choice of two toilets, two basins, and two bidets. His and hers, I thought. A giant bath sat in the centre of the room. One wall was a mirror—it was all rather distracting.

I saw another door and thoughts of escape resurfaced. It was locked.

I sat down to think.

She's very pretty. Well, more stunning. No, that implied a certain air-head quality which was clearly not present. There was a cat-like intelligence—and then I realised: her hair, last night it had been long and dark, today it was short and spiky, and—red. Yes, definitely red.

I wondered what she would want and suddenly a combination of my as-yet undone business, the thought of her and the anxiety combined to make a much firmer problem, not altogether unpleasant, but almost immediately ruined by the realisation that she was standing in the doorway looking at me. Her eyes held clear amusement.

"Will this take long?" she enquired. The Scottish accent was definitely there, but gentle—maybe she had lived down here a long time.

I noticed her gaze was not exactly centred on my eye level. I spluttered, trying to close my legs, do my business, and tuck away interested parties all in one movement, but had little success in any of these. I certainly couldn't *go* in this state.

"Please!" I managed, with as much dignity as I could. She snorted, and turned back into the bedroom.

A few minutes later, I returned to find her lying on the bed with my trousers scrunched up beside her. She had obviously finished with my phone, and was now going through my wallet.

"That's private," I tried. Another snort.

She pulled out my driving licence.

"James Glass. That's nice." She tried it out: "James, Jimmy, Jim ... James! What a lovely name!" The pause had been imperceptibly short, but I had heard it. I shuddered. My mother had strong thoughts about abbreviating names—which is probably why she had never thought to sound mine out. Usually, at least a raised eyebrow was called for—the reference would not have been lost on her, but she did not go for the obvious.

It was at that moment I thought I first fell for her. Later I realised it had been back at the bus shelter, but right then, watching her on the bed, my few possessions scattered around her, I was completely helpless as I felt emotions I had never felt before.

"Date of birth?" She looked carefully at my face as though to check some hidden counter in my forehead against the plastic card in her hand. "Eyes: grey"—she stretched forward to check—"hmm, maybe more like light blue with amber centres."

"Grey was easier to write."

"Address:" She digested this information with a slight nod.

"And who do you *work for,* Mr Glass?" Her voice hardened slightly, pulling my eyes back to hers like a fish on a hook. I felt like a very guilty fish.

"Work for? No one," and then, realising how unpalatable that was to myself, I added somewhat defensively: "I was, I mean I'm not always unemployed."

"So you don't work for Pharmaply?" I shook my head, a little wildly, unsure where this was going.

"Nor for Zolotran?" I continued to shake my head.

She broke eye contact as she thought about something, tapping my licence with her finger as she did so.

"Hmm, so how come you just happened to be waiting at *that* bus stop?"

I managed to shake off the feeling of guilt she engendered. Besides, I hadn't *done* anything, I reminded myself.

"Well how else was I going to get home? I was just waiting for the bus, minding my own business ..." I trailed off. She smiled and, after a moment, relaxed.

"Well done Mr Glass, you passed the test."

"A test? A test of what?"

"You are very observant, and I had to know you weren't looking for *me*.

However, we still have a problem. I left my car and my bag

back there and we have to go and get them."

"We?" I sputtered. I wasn't sure how the plural had entered this conversation.

"Well, are you going to make me go by myself, James?" Helena blinked a few times in quick succession as though holding back tears. I wasn't going to be taken in.

'That girl is trouble,' I heard my Nan say, even though she had never said it to me. I decided to deflect.

"Look," I said "of course I'd love to help, but I was going to go back to town to look for a job—"

"Wonderful!" she cut me off, "that's settled then! I'll hire you for the day. You can help me and then you won't need to look for a job because you'll have one!"

Only for a day, I thought.

"£500?" she asked. I stared. No one had ever offered me that for a *day*. I was suddenly wary.

"It's nothing illegal, is it?" It sounded feeble, even as I asked.

She looked deeply offended. "Of course not!" I noticed she did not elaborate.

I considered my options—which came down to going with her, and probably ending up in trouble, or finding my way back to the city centre to sit in the cafe all day, spending the last of my cash surfing for a job, and drinking Leon's disgusting tea.

I sighed. Somehow trouble sounded the better of the two options. Mr Cautious was outraged, so I made a play to placate him.

"Cash?"

"Of course!"

I was sold, and probably had been since ... well, since last night. The reality hit and I felt both elation and trepidation wander sinuously along my spine like embracing lovers.

"Okay," I tried to shrug nonchalantly, "and how are we going to get there?" I thought this might start to answer the question of where we were.

"You can drive, can't you?" She waved the licence and her rising eyebrows caused the lovers across my back to upgrade to a tango.

"Of course!" I tried to sound casual, but it had been a while.

"Get ready," she threw me the trousers. "If we hurry, we might still get breakfast."

She got up, stretched like a lazy cat, and headed for the bathroom, removing her top as she went. I sort of closed my eyes, but as she rolled her arms, I found myself admiring the way her shoulder blades moved so lithely under her tanned skin.

She turned, catching me with my eyes at exactly the wrong level. Or the right one, depending on your point of view. Or points of view. I stopped myself, looked up into her eyes, which again held that same faint amusement. "Oh, there's a spare toothbrush and anything else you need in the cabinet to the right of the basin." She turned, disappeared, and didn't close the door.

"Basins," I corrected her, in an attempt to regain some control.

I wasn't sure on protocol here. It seemed wrong to enter a girl's bathroom uninvited, but then she had *sort of* invited me. I compromised by drinking my tea, allowing her time to do any personal business. Then, I procrastinated by waiting a bit longer, and then I walked carefully to the door. I knocked loudly enough to claim that I had, but quietly enough so as not to scare her off, got no response, and entered, trying to look nonchalant.

"Hi!" I said brightly.

The effect was wasted on the empty room. A towel on the floor was the only evidence she had been there.

I found a toothbrush in the cabinet. I also found shower gel. I looked around for the shower and realised that what I had taken to be an alcove was just an entrance to the second half of the bathroom.

There were four main shower heads, and countless other taps and pipes and nozzles. I reckoned I had seen smaller car washes, and certainly ones with fewer jets.

A tile glowed under one of the shower heads. I reached out for it and was rewarded with a stream of warm water. The tile displayed more information. My hand played with the icons and I found the controls for temperature, flow, and pulse. This would take some time to master.

I looked around for a towel. The alcove had a rail of them, big, fluffy, white, and incredibly sensuous. One of them was missing.

As I towelled myself dry, I thought: next time, to hang with protocol, I'm not waiting.

4 – The Cat who Cooked Breakfast

As I dressed, I considered my options. Part of me considered that doing a swift runner was still viable. A house like this must have many points of exit, not the least of which would be the front door. I could probably just walk out without her seeing.

I also remembered just a few hours earlier, standing in a bus shelter feeling somewhat sorry for myself. I was so familiar with that state that I didn't even have to bemoan it. It sat on me like a well-worn jumper. Here I was, one short sleep later, having been through more emotion than I had experienced in a year. For the first time in a long while, maybe forever, I was anxious about more than just where my next meal was coming from, and it felt *good*. I could feel an almost solid knot in my stomach and it wasn't unpleasant—the best way to describe it was a *growl*.

I knew I had to stay. 'You'll regret it', Mr Cautious announced, but even he conceded that a small penalty would be worth it for having this much fun.

I stuck my head out of the bedroom door and looked both ways. I decided to go left. From there it wasn't hard to find my way downstairs—I just followed the ever widening passageway. The walls were bright and clean, rendered in white, but with bulges and cracks that spoke of older beginnings.

I descended a wider and more luxurious staircase than last night. It opened into an entrance hall covered in small tiles coloured black, terracotta, and butter-cream. They were tessellated into a geometry that managed not to compete with the stair carpet. One end of the hall showed a thin partition of blood-red and Bristol-blue glass, set in a simple off-white wooden frame. It divided the main hall from the front door and I realised my chance to leave was straight ahead. I took a step towards the partition.

"Georgian. With Victorian 'improvements'."

I turned in time to see the air quotes disappear. I wasn't sure which of the improvements she was unhappy with—the house was amazing as far as I had seen, and if I lived here, I certainly wouldn't quibble about the architecture.

I tried not to stare as Helena continued her descent. She wore ox-blood leather trousers and a simple white blouse that failed to conceal the cobalt blue of her bra. I had expected heels, but she was in Dr Martens. She carried a briefcase in one hand and a pair of dark glasses in the other. Her hair was now blonde.

"Come on."

We entered the dining room through a redwood-panelled door. At one end, large folding doors obscured the room or rooms beyond, while at the other, an almost floor-to-ceiling bay window revealed a well-ordered and lushly filled garden, complete with steps to an upper level and a fountain.

The heavy oak table was dressed with a white tablecloth and laid with three place settings, although there were four chairs each side, with space for more. A few toast crumbs suggested we were not the first to use them, but the silverware was clean. Against the inner wall was a long sideboard. Silver-covered dishes hinted at an elegant breakfast.

Helena placed her briefcase on the floor and picked up two plates, passing one to me.

"Help yourself," she said, so I did, and we sat down.

I smiled at Helena as I bit into a particularly good sausage.

Helena smiled back. "We grow them here."

"Oh, you have pigs?" It took me a moment. The garden must be bigger than I could see.

"Yes, Alex keeps them." I wondered if Alex was the hired help or the husband. Or both. I used a few mouthfuls to contemplate the possibilities, and went back for more beans.

I made good progress on the rest of the sausages, and I was

starting to wonder about the possibility of a fried egg when the thought was cut short by the squeak of a shoe. I looked up in time to see a pair of lime-green plimsolls walk through the door on the feet of a blonde fairy carrying two plates.

Not a fairy, I recalculated: judging from the almond oval of her face, an elf. I found myself looking at the tips of her ears and then feeling guilty as she smiled at me. Every single part of her, from her hands to her smile, seemed scaled to a perfect three-quarter-size human. Helena did the introductions.

"James, this is Cleo. Cleo, James."

Cleo smiled, and held out two large plates.

"Fried or scrambled?"

"Um, fried please." Cleo placed two perfectly done eggs in front of me, and put the scrambled in front of Helena. "Careful, they're hot," she warned. She wiped her hand on her apron and then offered it to me.

"Hello James, I'm cook, housekeeper, and bottle washer." We shook hands, me bobbing my head up and down as I swallowed a final mouthful of sausage. She laughed. Her laugh was unexpectedly deep.

She crossed to the dresser and brought over the bacon tureen, placing it in front of us. "Help yourselves." She stole a piece herself, and wandered around the table to sit on Helena's other side, opposite me. Apparently the housekeeper was welcome at the breakfast table.

"Oh, I forgot the tea." Another laugh, and she was gone.

Helena was watching me closely. I felt my cheeks redden as I understood she knew the effect Cleo was having on me. She looked amused, but held back, as though waiting for a punchline.

The elf reappeared, and placed a pot of tea in front of me. "Thanks, Cleo," I said, trying not to look too hard at her. Helena laughed out loud.

Somewhat embarrassed, I looked down and saw that inexplicably the elf's distinctive shoes had changed from green and were now a fetching shade of pink. Puzzled, I lifted my eyes to her face and she spoke.

"Actually, I'm Cat." A moment passed, and then she added helpfully, "We're twins."

The voice was identical too, so I wasn't convinced by the twins story. I wasn't sure if this was some elaborate game cooked up by her and Helena, but I couldn't see any reason for them to be trying to fool me, apart from the value of the initial joke.

"James, this is Cat."

Cat leaned over and kissed me on the cheek. It was a very friendly kiss. She straightened and bounced over to Helena, landing on her lap. This time the kiss was even more friendly.

Helena caught my eye as they broke contact. Cat headed out, but looked over her shoulder at me and giggled as she left.

"They seem nice," I said lamely. Helena smiled again.

"You'll find they are very competent if you get to know them."

"I'm sure," I started, but at that moment Cat reappeared carrying a teapot, and Cleo, the teacups. After a moment I realised I had to swap them again. Cleo equals green, Cat equals pink, I reminded myself. 'Longer name, longer colour,' Mr Logical supplied. The girls sat opposite me after a little tussle as both tried to sit closest to Helena.

As one of them poured the tea, I searched their faces for some dissimilarity. Usually identical twins aren't too identical. I looked for facial blemishes, birthmarks, pierced ears, earrings, different hair, but I found nothing. Each sported short, tousled, almost white hair which faded into very pale skin, and both appeared devoid of piercings, let alone earrings. Another glance confirmed that both sets of bright, intelligent eyes were the same shade of hazel flecked with green, which only enhanced their elfin nature.

"Excuse me, James," one of them said. "We just need to ask

Helena …" They both turned and looked serious.

"Helena, you know you said we should paint the ceiling white?"

"Yes, Cleo."

"Well, would it be sooo bad if it was a pale blue?"

"The palest, palest blue you can imagine," added Cat.

"It's just it would be like looking at the sky, then."

"And we might add some clouds."

"No clouds." Helena's tone was firm, but I smiled as I understood the old sales tactic they had pulled—selling her on the minor point.

Cleo squealed. "So we can paint it blue, then?"

Helena realised she had been had, and gave in, good-naturedly. She tried to recoup some ground. "I need to see the colour first. And if it looks awful when it's on, then you have to repaint it white, okay?"

The twins nodded, looking pleased with themselves, and turned their attention back to me.

"Finished?" they spoke together, weirdly stereophonic.

"So remind me who cooks," I asked, hopeful of separating them.

"Cat cooked today, and I washed up." Okay, so that's Cleo on the right.

"But we sort of take it in turns. And sometimes we do it together."

"Well, thank you, that was the best breakfast I've had in a long time." A very long time, I thought.

The twins graciously inclined their heads. Helena shooed them off on the pretext of wanting to talk business, but then helped herself to another cup of tea and sat staring at it thoughtfully.

I remembered 'the problem' she had mentioned and decided silence was my best ally. She looked up, smiled as though she had forgotten I was there, and took a final swallow.

I stole a scrap of bacon, and she smiled. “Thank you, breakfast.” I wondered if she always thanked her breakfast, and she caught my look, and with a shrug dismissed it. “An old friend.”

I wasn’t completely satisfied, but she distracted me.

“Ready?”

For what? I thought, but I just nodded. She retrieved her briefcase, found a jacket, and led the way. I followed.

Her leather trousers were really very well tailored.

5 – Studies in Black and Blue

We exited the dining room the way we had come, but rather than use the front entrance, Helena headed further into the house.

As I passed the door to what looked like the kitchen, I couldn't resist a peek. Long beech-block counter tops lined the walls, covering off-white cabinets, all neatly closed. A deep burgundy range sat against the far wall. Beside it was an array of cooking implements. I looked, but saw no sign of either elf. *Twin*, I corrected. Cleo and Cat. Or Cat and Cleo.

We left the house the same way we had entered last night. We passed what could be stables, and some other stone outbuildings enclosing a cobbled courtyard. We circled the yard and entered a low doorway that broke a deep stone wall of least two storeys high.

I was not shocked by the proportions of the garage in what once must have been a barn—size in this house no longer surprised me. Instead of bare slate, there was a ceiling. The contrast of white plaster and oak beam was not unlike a country church, but here the objects of worship were hunched all around me on the garage floor—cars to die for.

As my eyes grew accustomed to the gloom, I spotted a couple of bangers looking out of place. To the left was a wide multi-panelled door, gleaming in a streak of sunlight with a newish coat of British Racing Green. Close to it were a couple of very utilitarian white vans, and a minibus or two. Apart from the anachronisms, everything else brooded with a menace that said 'don't get too close'. If I had been wearing a hat, I would have removed it in reverence.

And then I saw *her*. Slightly behind a blue minibus so I had not seen her at first. I had to cross half the floor to get a better angle: a *Veyron Bleu*. '*A Grand Sport,*' Mr Logical corrected me, 'the top is off'.

I ignored him as I stared. I had downloaded the Bugatti

Bleu Centenaire with its startling bright sapphire paintwork as my laptop screen-saver one day at Leon's cafe. Sapphire? Or was it cobalt? I remembered the hint of colour beneath Helena's blouse.

From somewhere outside came the distinctive sound of something kicking over a metal pail. Several times or several pails, it sounded like. I turned.

Helena was looking very guilty. "Wait here," she commanded, "choose a car." Her flapping hand told me to stay in the garage as she put down her case and jacket and turned, running back the way we had come.

Sounds of an argument erupted from quite close by. Or at least a one-sided argument. I couldn't hear words, but I didn't think it was Helena shouting.

I sank slowly into the driver's seat of the Bugatti. Very classy, apart from some blue furry dice hanging from the rear-view mirror. Not to my taste, but I thought if one could afford a car like this, one could afford to have a poor taste in accessories. The key was in, and the radio simple enough to operate. Someone liked Radio 3, but it wasn't enough to cover the shouting and clatter of ironmongery.

I gave the dice a tap with my finger in a friendly sort of way and then sat quickly upright as I was reprimanded. 'Mind the hair, man.' I managed to stop myself looking around to find the source of the words. Clearly the sound had come from the dice themselves. It sounded like Eddie Murphy. I tapped them again and was rewarded with a 'Keep cool, man. Keep cool!' I wondered how much Eddie Murphy dice cost.

There was more noises off. With a sigh, I thought I'd better at least look like I might help, so I turned off the radio and eased my way out of the sleek blue vehicle.

I exited the garage door in time to see a Rubenesque lass turn out of the stables and stride off into the house, her long black hair rippling across the back of the Gothic-like costume she wore. Helena half-followed and I heard her say "Sorry,

Celestine" to the retreating back. Helena stopped. It was interesting to see her looking contrite.

A pail was lying in the yard and Helena retrieved it with lowered shoulders and returned it to the stables. She glanced up and saw me and gave a wry grimace before straightening herself and walking over.

"Trouble?" I asked.

"Something I forgot." As she picked up her things I caught the naked pain on her face and decided not to press for details. Instead, I pointed to the Bugatti.

"Don't be silly, we can't go in that! What would they think?" Any contriteness had disappeared and the fiery Helena was back. She dumped two crates in the boot of a dark red Golf convertible, placed her briefcase and jacket on the back seat, and jumped in. "And I'm driving."

Sadly, I took the left-hand seat.

She took a deep breath, turned the key, and the engine turned over like an angry kitty. I found myself thinking this might not be a standard Golf.

"Cabriolet," she explained, "with some 'mods'"—again the air quotes. She reversed carefully into the central aisle and as we moved towards the far end, the green doors opened, concertinaing to the side. Wide enough for a tank.

"We need to get you a suit," she announced, "so, shopping first. Then I've got a few errands, and then you can get to work. Maybe a spot of lunch." Helena moved her sunglasses down from her forehead.

I didn't need any food at that moment, but the thought of another meal in hand, a good suit, maybe a clean shirt, and lunch with a beautiful woman, not to mention £500 cash, all seemed like a dream date.

'Unless you get blown up,' Mr Grumpy muttered.

6 – Antipasto

After the gentle and precise easing out of the garage, I was unprepared for the full-throated roar as Helena floored the pedal and we hurtled down the driveway. I tightened my seatbelt, but slowly, so as not to let her see.

After a short distance the gravel gave way to a paved avenue, lined with beech. The curves were gentler now. I didn't want to look at the speedometer, mainly for fear of the knowledge, and partly to prevent offence, but it took us a couple of minutes to reach the end of the avenue. We roared through the gates and Helena turned onto the road so forcefully I was lifted out of my seat. We crested a small hill and the main road lay before us.

The highway seemed to restore her mood somewhat, and we settled down to a speed that wouldn't offend any speed cameras. The sun was doing its best, but some clouds were hovering on the horizon. Perhaps last night's rain would return.

I now recognised the bus route, but I couldn't figure out where we had been dropped off the previous night. It certainly hadn't been at the front gate. I wanted to ask Helena about the blond hair, but she picked up her phone and pressed a button. The sounds of a call being connected came over the car's speakers.

"Pharma Inspectorate." The voice wasn't friendly.

"I'm very sorry," was all Helena said, and she hung up. I thought it was strange to get a wrong number from speed dial, but she let the phone drop into the cradle, and took a deep breath.

Helena drove purposefully, staring straight ahead. As we neared the city, the traffic began to increase, and we had to slow. Her frown turned into a scowl.

In contrast I felt quite pleased with myself—riding in an adolescent-sounding car, sun up, top down, and a gorgeous blonde driving. I tried to look as if I did this every day.

Helena was still a bit heavy on the acceleration and the growl meant people were looking at us. At her. My boss; my chauffeur; my colleague; my girlfriend—I tried out the various titles, unsure which I preferred, and, more importantly, which ones she might allow. I figured girlfriend was a bit optimistic, but then this time yesterday, driving in a car would have been optimistic.

The traffic slowed again and Helena impatiently wrenched the wheel, turning off the main route, to roar down a side road. A few minutes later we were back on the main road. It seemed to me we had not made much progress—I was sure the same van was still ahead of us.

We passed the shelter where we had met, not so many hours earlier, but Helena didn't even give it a glance as she turned off the road, and we raced down a back street toward some industrial units.

She more or less parked the car in front of a sign that read 'Digital Art—Printing and Beyond'. I wasn't sure what digital art was, and I didn't get to find out as she said 'Please stay here' in a tone that suggested arguing would be pointless. Ten minutes later she emerged and we were on our way again.

***

I've always hated clothes shopping. Too much traipsing around indecisively and too many choices available.

I thought this trip might be like that, but there was a difference. Whereas my mum had always looked at stuff before asking me "Do you like this?" Helena just glanced, held things up, and made a decision.

If she didn't like the garment, she replaced it carefully on the rack. If she did then she said "This" and handed it to me. Shopping is easy when a person knows what they want.

It took minutes for her to select the items, and another fifteen for me to try them on, while she swapped out the trousers for a slightly larger pair. She made me parade outside the changing rooms and pose for a photo on her phone: new suit, belt, shirt, blue tie, and black lace-up shoes. She pronounced herself happy, sent me back to change out of them.

As she paid, I noticed she had added two other shirts, some boxers, socks, and a red tie. It seemed a lot of clothes for one day. The assistant greeted her like an old friend, and when Helena asked if she could leave the bags for a while, they were tucked away with a note. We left, again empty handed, except for her purse.

I followed her thoughtfully. I had to admit the suit had looked good, and hadn't been cheap. I wondered if I had wanted more say in which suit had been chosen. I decided this was business, and for £500 I would gladly wear any suit the lady wanted.

Our next stop was a barber; she led me inside. "Short back and sides, please," she asked, "and clean shaven, no sideburns." I didn't argue as the young stylist efficiently carried out the order.

We left, Helena walking in front smiling to herself absent-mindedly, before asking for another quick photo. I followed, the cool air washing over my face.

We passed several shops and then stopped suddenly outside a bakery.

"We need to kill some time." Helena looked at her watch again. "It's a bit early for lunch. Do you like ducks, James?"

I wasn't sure. I certainly liked the crispy kind, with pancakes, but I suspected that the plural meant the living variety. I shrugged.

***

Helena strode into the bakery, selected four multi-seed baps, and, emerging, she pointed at a footbridge at the far end of the shops. At her pace it didn't take long to walk, and as we crested the bridge I saw a park with a lake, woodchip-covered paths and a few swings in an enclosed play area. On the lake swam some unsuspecting ducks. And swans.

Walking towards the part of the lake with swans, Helena cut across the grass which still felt a bit squelchy underfoot. I realised how practical her boots were.

We sat on the bench, beside a sign asking us not to feed bread to the wildlife. She handed me a roll, and then took one herself, breaking off a small bit to throw to one of last year's cygnets. Other swans immediately gathered round, and I watched as she accurately landed a morsel in front of each beak, favouring the younger birds.

"So," she said, as she turned towards me, "tell me about yourself, Gym Class."

The softness and the little smile that brushed her lips removed any sting from the words. Her tone said she was teasing, and the little shove she gave as she moved closer told me that she was holding me with care. I smiled, acknowledging the well-worn pun, and wondered where to start.

"I'm twenty-eight. I grew up with my mum in a village not far from where I now live. My dad bunked off soon after I was born. We did okay. I went to uni in Brum to study psychology. Dropped out after a year when I discovered I didn't really like people that much. But while I was there I found I got on okay with machines; picked up some computer skills; and now I do bits and bobs for people. Networks, admin, databases. Some programming."

"Which databases?" I was slightly taken aback. I had never encountered anyone outside work who had asked this.

"Um, lots. Oracle and mySql mainly these days, but older ones too." I was warming to this girl who understood my small corner of the universe.

"And you live at home?"

"Yes. I mean, no, not my mum's, I have my own place." I looked away, thinking of her Georgian with Victorian 'improvements' pile. I decided a bit more honesty might be called for. "Well, someone's garage, really. It's out in the sticks, so it's cheap."

I didn't mention that it also had no Wi-Fi, nor that the internet in the main house was so slow as to not really qualify for the term 'broadband'.

"I come into town to look for jobs ... and to get better web access." I shrugged to indicate it was no big deal.

"So then, a loner who is good with computers?"

"Well, not so much a loner," I said, not wanting to give the impression that I hated people *that* much. "It's more like," I hesitated and she filled the space with just the right word:

"Alone."

I turned back to her; she was looking out across the water. I couldn't really tell from her profile, but there may have been a slight quiver.

"Well, yes. Basically." I finished somewhat lamely, and so had another go: "People are ... difficult." It sounded just as pitiful.

"Difficult, as in you find yourself biting your tongue a lot." Her face was expressionless, the dark glasses hid her eyes.

"Yes. Sort of like they all went to a different school."

Helena smiled. "A different school, *and* on a different planet." I laughed; she was right.

"James," she continued, "maybe you're just—" she hesitated for a moment, not searching for the word, because I saw her catch herself—she was trying to break it to me gently—"just different." She was looking far away again. I nodded, feeling naked.

"One company said I wasn't a team player," I admitted.

She snorted. "If you want team players, look no further than your average sheep."

She took another roll, indicated the flock in front of us, and threw a bit. She looked at my unbroken roll and then at the birds as though to say I was letting the side down.

So I threw bread. The sun shone. The girl beside me

seemed to understand me, but I knew that it was just a matter of time before natural selection separated us. I closed my eyes against the sun and let the day wash over me.

***

Helena elbowed me.

"Come on, time to go."

"Where are we going?" I asked.

"Back to the printers." She emptied the last crumbs into the lake and we walked in silence back to the car park. This time she gave me the driving seat, and showed me how to lower the roof. I retraced our route as far as I could from memory while Helena lay back, absorbing the sun.

I waited in the car outside at the printers, but this time only for a minute. Helena emerged with a thick A4 envelope which she put in her briefcase behind me. As she climbed back in, she placed a small metal business card holder in her jacket pocket, looking most pleased with herself.

"And now lunch," she announced.

***

It was a good lunch, but as we returned to the shop where we had left our purchases, I felt an impending sense of doom.

I used the fitting rooms to change into my suit, emerging with my old clothes in a bag.

I had looked at myself all ways in the mirrors and with the haircut and shave I told myself I could tackle anything. Helena looked pleased, and as we walked back to the car she hooked her arm though mine.

"Time for work," she purred.

I felt another tug of tension within, and Mr Grumpy reminded me that there was no such thing as a free lunch.

7 – Easy Money

Helena decided to drive again and since she knew where we were going, I was happy to let her. The softness that she had shown earlier was still apparent, but I could sense it fading as we hit the main road.

The bus shelter appeared ahead of us. It had looked drab the night before—now it just looked ordinary. I couldn't help but turn my head, wondering if some magical portal had manifested itself there. How else to account for the sudden shift in my well-being? Sure, this job was only for the day, but it was proving to be a wonderful day.

'At least so far,' Mr Cautious reminded me. I was well aware of the free lunch syndrome, and I had tacitly agreed with myself that I would probably now need to pay in some way. I just wished I knew how.

The sun, the lunch, the beautiful girl had all worked their magic, and I was starting to feel more confident. Mr Grumpy and Mr Cautious, however, had not abandoned me, and they alternately reminded me there was a big difference between feeling reckless and *being* reckless.

Helena had said almost nothing about herself all morning. The purr she had given as we left the car park had sounded as though she was looking forward to whatever this work was. A few blocks later, we turned left and entered a business park.

The campus was leafy and the road paved with expensive bricks. Either side of the carriageway was lined with bicycle lanes and walkways. A few employees, suited and briefcased, were sauntering along, sipping from paper coffee cups—not in a hurry, even though lunch was long over.

We turned into a car park. A man in overalls was polishing a brass plaque mounted on a sturdy brick pillar built solely to hold the sign. It said 'Pharmaply', plus some tag line I didn't have time to read. I remembered that Helena had mentioned the name when she was going through my things this morning.

Clearly Pharmaply was doing well enough to have ample space for its employees and visitors. I could see several spots much closer to the building, but she chose a place some distance away.

"That's my car," she said as she got out. She pointed to a silver Japanese car of indeterminate age parked two spaces away. I stared, trying to connect the two disparate styles of car, her banger and this sports car.

She called me round to the back of the Golf. Her briefcase was open. She pulled out a lanyard with a laminated card, and slipped it over my neck.

She turned back to the boot. I picked up the badge, but before I could read it, she handed me a pair of thick spectacles. "Put these on." My vision became bowl-like. "Look down a bit, keep your eyes central, and you'll be able to see," she suggested. I did so, and there was a small circle of focus.

I picked up the badge, but it was too blurry to read. An ID card of some kind. I tried the glasses out on the cars instead, and as my head swam I decided it was best not to try looking too hard.

"Come here."

I wobbled over to her. She took my shoulders with both hands and leaned in, licking her lips as she did so. Protocol again deserted me—it seemed an odd time and place for a kiss and so I froze; even shut my eyes. Her lips did not touch mine, but instead locked onto the side of my neck. She kissed me, long and full; I felt her tongue working its way around.

My rudimentary knowledge of such things suggested this was the wrong spot and wrong time, but still it felt nice and tingly. I wondered if I should do the same and started to lean in to her neck when, just as quickly, she broke off and stood to one side. I turned my head to better focus on her, but she twisted my chin back and I felt her other hand press something against my skin. She counted to ten, and then peeled it back. "There!" she exclaimed as she took a vanity mirror from the boot and showed me my brand-new neck tattoo—a somewhat wonky skull.

I wondered how much of the kiss had been necessary to stick the tattoo on. Then I wondered how long I could avoid washing that part of me. I was also trying to figure out if that was the closest I'd got to being kissed by someone other than a relative.

My thoughts were interrupted as she pulled my hand towards hers. "Here are the keys." She pointed again to the silver car.

"Now, listen carefully."

Here it comes, I thought. Messrs Cautious, Grumpy, and Logical all pulled up front-row seats.

"When I send you, go to the big red skip behind the building and find my bag." She showed me a picture of a small green rucksack. "Then, get in the car," she pointed to the grey Toyota, "and drive it home. Wait for me at home."

I nodded and repeated: "Red skip; green bag; go home." I lifted the glasses to get a better look at the photo of the bag.

"When you get home, if you get a chance, there's a plastic bag in my rucksack with floppy disks. Have a quick squint at them." She was suddenly very serious. It sounded simple enough, and not particularly illegal.

"How do I find my way back to your place?" I was a bit nervous of the last few miles.

I heard again the condescending voice she had used the night before.

"Glove compartment. Satnav. Press Home." Her eyebrows asked if I had managed to follow this complex sequence. I nodded.

"And don't speed. The last thing we need is a nosy traffic cop." I nodded, as though I understood, but I didn't know why.

She motioned me back into the sporty Golf, and we drove

up to the front of the building. She parked ostentatiously. We got out and put on our jackets. "Right! Walk tall, look like you're meant to be here." She followed her own instructions and we set off towards the front door.

***

It's a good thing that glass is made from sand, because if it were made from trees, then an entire rainforest would have given its life for the façade of Pharmaply's 'Divisional Development Centre'. The thick spectacles gave it an ethereal, almost ocean-like quality. If I kept my head very still and concentrated, I could see just about enough. The peering probably made me look short-sighted.

A vertical slice of five floors was dedicated to the lobby. The marble floor was emblazoned with the company logo and at the far end was a curved glass counter as long as a railway carriage. Behind this structure sat a single receptionist, the slab of glass serving as her desk, on which sat a single phone and a computer screen.

Beyond her, there was more glass, mostly frosted this time, shielding the inner workings of the building. Large arches into this barrier housed security apparatus that would happily have serviced a small airport.

Helena strode up to the desk.

"Good morning, I'd like to see Mr Wuthers please." She placed a card on the desk.

The receptionist tried hard to find a reason not to pick up the card, but then stretched to do so. After a glance, she straightened slightly, dialled, paused, and looked over her glasses at Helena. She did passive-aggressive very well, I thought. She sat up even straighter as the call was answered.

"My Wuthers, this is Dawn in Reception. I have an Emma Vaughn here from the Department."

My eyes widened at the name, but luckily I was facing the coffee table in the waiting area. The noise from the other end of the phone was interesting—a possible expletive turned rapidly into coughing. The receptionist replaced the receiver and said very formally: "Please take a seat, he'll be right down." I followed Helena to the waiting area.

'Right down' turned out to be twenty-five minutes. As we sat, I was thankful that the chairs were not also made of glass. A smattering of industry journals lay in neat piles, the shareholder news prominent among them.

A large TV screen to the side was silently displaying a rolling set of slides about Pharmaply. It gave me a headache to look, so I pretended to be happy just staring at the table.

Helena picked up a journal to read. A few minutes later she slipped it into her briefcase. While I was pondering this unexpected kleptomania, she appeared to change her mind, reached in and replaced the publication on the desk. I was about to ask her what was so interesting that it warranted removal, when she picked the thing up again and approached the translucent slab.

"Do you have another copy of this that I could take away please?"

Miss Passive-Aggressive took the proffered journal as Helena continued. "It's just that I notice there's an job advert on the back for our department, and I'm not sure it's been advertised internally yet."

Dawn in Reception clearly knew how to handle requests like this. Hardly glancing at the glossy cover she said, "Oh no, I'm sorry, this is the only one. We have to keep one down here for Health and Safety."

The way she said 'Health and Safety' suggested there was no arguing with this point. She put the journal firmly down on her desk, just out of Helena's reach.

I was slightly outraged at this behaviour, but since I was still unsure what we were doing there, I refrained from saying anything. Helena returned and sat down. She didn't look at all upset by these bad manners. I wondered if that was why she had thought about just stealing it.

It was at this point that a short, red-faced man, with shirt tails not quite tucked in, approached through the barriers. His hair was thinning and he brushed his fingers through it, rearranging his florid face into a smile. I got the impression that he was trying hard to look benevolent.

"Ms Vaughn? Bill Wuthers. *So* sorry to keep you waiting, I was just checking a security shipment." They shook hands. Helena turned to me.

"This is my assistant Nicholas Jones. We're here to do an unannounced inspection." Mr Wuthers smiled broadly, but I noticed his brow was damp.

"Of course, of course. It's just ..." He was trying to stall, and looked around as though the glass sea would give him some inspiration. The silence was about to get embarrassing when his eyes finally widened with an idea. "Ah! You don't mind if we call your office, do you? It's now policy to check all visitors. I'm *very* sorry." He tried to look sorry, but failed, the brilliance of his idea obviously appealing to him.

"A very good policy, Mr Wuthers." Helena offered her phone. "I have them here on speed dial."

"Oh please, call me Bill," the smile widened alarmingly, "and if you don't mind, we have to use our own phone. Policy." The elegant shrug reiterated his sorrow. Helena nodded, and helpfully produced another business card. But Mr Wuthers wasn't biting. "Ah yes, please don't worry, I'll ask Dawn to dial."

He looked at Dawn of Reception, who had undergone a miraculous metamorphosis. Passive-Aggressive Girl had vanished and had been replaced by Ever-So-Helpful Girl.

"The number for the Department please?" Mr Wuthers asked.

The girl smiled righteously—someone caught in the right place at the right time—and passed across the journal Helena had been reading, pointing at the advert. He nodded, and she dialled. He waved his finger and she turned on the phone's speaker.

One ring later the phone was answered: "Pharma Inspectorate, how may I direct your call?" It was the same voice as earlier, but now sounding so much happier. I wondered if all receptionists suffered from psychological problems. Bill Wuthers drew himself up.

"Good morning. Do you have an Emma Vaughn, please?"

"Ms Vaughn is one of our senior inspectors, but I'm afraid she is out of the office today. May I put you through to her voicemail, or I could give you her mobile?"

"Her mobile would be perfect please."

Miss Ever-So-Helpful wrote it down, and then dialled. Helena's phone began to ring. Bill decided he had wasted enough of our time and gestured to Dawn, who hung up.

"I'm so sorry, Ms Vaughn, we do have to be *so* careful. Why just yesterday we had a potential security breach!"

"Yes," said Helena, "that is why we are here." Our wait was amply paid for by the panicked expression on the red face. He regained control with difficulty.

"Of course, of course, please come on up." He bowed. Helena stopped him with a hand, opened her briefcase and removed a yellow bin bag.

"Excuse me a moment." She nodded at Wuthers and turned to me, handing over the bag.

"Mr Jones," she addressed me, and I remembered my new name in time to look interested. "Please go and check the waste management around the back of the building. We're looking for poor document control—things that should be shredded but aren't. Best to get a representative sample from the admin skip."

I noticed that as she handed me the bag, she was looking at Wuthers. He looked serene. I saw the slightest frown appear above Helena's sunglasses.

She rummaged further in her briefcase, and pulled out a paper mask and what looked like a squashed marker pen. It had a little indicator panel on the side. “Use the mask and biohazard chemical trace meter before you touch anything,” her voice commanded. Now Wuthers was looking unhappy.

I had to stop myself from bowing too, but instead, I nodded sagely, put on the mask, and walked out the front door. As I turned to follow the side of the building, I saw Helena and Wuthers pass through into the translucent inner-sanctum. My glasses made it look like a movie dissolve.

I removed them once I was out of sight of reception but in doing so, I noticed a little pod of a CCTV camera high on the outside wall. I made a show of cleaning the lenses instead, before replacing them on my nose.

No one stopped me as I strolled around the perimeter. At the back of the building was the usual collection of skips, tired tarmac, and loading bays. I had to ‘clean’ my glasses again in order to locate the giant skip marked ‘Admin Waste Only’. I walked around it, looking for a way in. Luckily it had a side door. The screech of steel on steel greeted me as I worked the rusty door bolt. With an ungraceful whine, the door opened and I could see inside. Thankfully it was almost empty.

I took out the pen, and waved it around. The meter showed a smiley face, so I assumed it was safe to continue, although some instructions would have been nice. As a second thought I removed the cap and stuck the tip into the nearby heap of paper. I left it for a minute, and when the smiley remained, I tried for five more. Satisfied as far as I could be, I replaced the cap, put the device back inside my jacket, and stepped inside. I had to lift my glasses to look around.

A green rucksack was lying just inside the open end of the skip, slightly obscured by some printout. I was aware of a faint smell, so I trod carefully and, using a piece of paper as a glove, picked up the rucksack and dropped it into the yellow bag. I added some shredded and unshredded paper for completeness.

I paused, and listened. Nothing happened.

Replacing the glasses, I exited the skip, and shut the door as much as my ears would allow. Trying to look like I was 'meant to be there', I sauntered back to the old car.

I opened the boot, dumped the sack amongst an interesting collection of bric-a-brac, and then made my way around to the driver's door. At first I thought the car had been burgled—the front seats looked like someone had been searching them for drugs. However, given that the doors were locked and the windows shut, I concluded this was how it had been left.

I sat down, and found that while there wasn't much of the original upholstery left, the padding was still very comfortable. The beat-up car had seen better days, I thought, but the engine started first time and murmured happily to itself as I dug out the satnav.

"Glove compartment. Satnav. Press Home." I tried to emulate Helena's tone.

A friendly female and definitely Scottish voice awoke from its silicon slumber, and guided me out of the car park. I drove carefully past the last sentinel camera and then thankfully ditched the glasses.

I opened up the throttle a bit as I hit the main road, and the car responded well, the beat-up look not reflected in the engine's smoothness. I was surprised at how good a drive it was, the cornering tight, the gears precise and smooth.

As I left the city, I wished that this car had a top to put down so I could enjoy the afternoon sun. I tried driving with the windows open, but it was too turbulent.

I remembered Helena's admonition about speed and kept just under the limit, enjoying the long curves of the country road as I was guided back towards to the house by the cheerful voice.

That was an easy £500 to earn, I thought, my happiness matching that of my navigator.

8 – Hidden Treasures

A few miles from the turn-off, as I passed a row of houses set back from the road, the satnav proudly announced that I had reached my destination. I slowed, somewhat puzzled, but then reckoned this could be a security feature in case the car fell into the wrong hands. Perhaps there was a good reason why 'home' didn't lead to home. Anyway, I knew the way from there, and soon I was enjoying the drive down the winding avenue to the house.

I pulled to a stop just outside the still open garage doors, got out, and stretched. Life felt good. I removed Helena's bag from the yellow sack, placed it on the beat-up bonnet, and opened it. Inside, as she had said, I found a clear zip-lock bag with over a dozen floppy disks. The three and a half inch kind, with their stiff plastic covers. I took one out; it was labelled but unmarked. I slid back the metal shield to reveal the dark brown magnetic material nestling inside the white dust covers.

As I was examining this obsolete storage media and was wondering how to read it, a side door to the garage opened and a dark-haired man stepped out, wiping his hands on a rag. I reckoned he was in his mid-thirties, and assumed this was the Alex that Helena had mentioned at breakfast.

"Hi, I'm James," I introduced myself.

"Marek," he responded. "Helena warned me you were coming." So this was not the pig keeper. His dark hair and somewhat round face hinted at an Eastern European heritage, which matched his softly accented voice.

I offered to move the car, but he told me to leave it where it was, as he had to make space for it later.

"Helena said you know about computers and stuff?" he continued, and when I nodded he added, "She thought you might be able to help me with a problem."

I agreed. After all, the £500 had been for a day, and so far all I had done was root around in a skip and drive home.

"Sure, what sort of problem?"

I followed Marek into the garage and past the cars, to the side, through some steel doors into an extension, parallel to the main garage but narrower.

It housed a workshop with a comprehensive collection of tools and equipment. The perimeter was lined with workbenches.

As we walked, I saw that not all of the kit was car related. One bench sported a standard high-level toilet cistern on its side, another had what I was sure was an old HP radio spectrum analyser, the size of a small fridge. A useful device to detect a wide range of transmissions, but not usually found in the countryside. The colour of this one suggested a military origin.

I looked up. Four large ceiling fans hung from the high beams, their five long blades currently dormant. The roof shared the same sort of in-fill ceiling as the main garage, except here it was held in place with chicken wire.

This area was a little warmer than the car area, and right in the centre of it was the Veyron, propped up on jacks, looking a little sad with its wheels off the ground.

"She's beautiful," I commented, and Marek nodded.

"You know about cars?" The accent on 'cars' was a little thicker.

I told him I was a novice, but I liked them. He stroked the Bugatti as though it were a pet.

"These are not easy to find, and they're certainly not cheap." He hesitated, but then straightened his shoulders as though he had decided to be more direct.

"Helena was given this one in payment for a job she did." He paused, thinking about his words.

I tried to remember what the *Grand Sport* cost, assuming you could find one. It had to be over a million. What sort of 'job' had Helena done? I had already figured out that the

Pharma Inspector thing was dodgy. Marek interrupted my analysis with something that didn't make me feel better:

"We think it must be trackered."

I looked at him, trying to play it cool. "So Helena acquired this car legitimately?" He nodded. "But, someone thinks it's hot?" Another nod. "And you can't find the tracker." Marek pursed his lips and shook his head, agreeing with me.

"I've tried everything. I mean, we have trackers in all our cars, so I expected something. There was even a standard tracker in the door which was easy to find, but we had been given the code for that and it had been disabled."

I gestured at some of the electronics kit lying about. "Can't you sniff around for it?"

"A better question," he said, "is how come the cops aren't here?"

Good point, I thought. Some thieves leave a stolen car parked up somewhere for a week to see if it's tracked. Cheaper than electronics. No cops here meant this device was more sophisticated. I looked at him to continue.

"It only goes off when it's been driven." He looked at me to see what I would make of this. I thought he was leading me by the nose to some predetermined conclusions, but the look suggested he was expecting more. I decided to play along.

"So it's on blocks to simulate driving?" My tone told him this seemed obvious, and he smiled indulgently.

"Yes," he nodded, "it's on blocks so you can satisfy yourself that it is not the wheels spinning that trigger the squawk. It has to be driving." I nodded too. "So far, I've figured out the trigger speed is 30 miles per hour. Keep it under that, no squawk. Go faster than that, and within thirty minutes the thing goes off.

"It's very clever though, it disarms as soon as you stop, so you can't use static equipment to detect it." He waved at the spectrum analyser. I doubted the fridge-like HP would even fit in the Bugatti, and in any case, it wouldn't be easy to carry the necessary mains power for it.

We went through more of the obvious ideas, and for good practice he loaded the 70 kilogram sack he used to simulate a driver's weight, and the nifty aluminium bracket he had gaffered together to keep the accelerator pressed. A threaded bar provided fine adjustment. He was just about to start her up when I asked:

"What about if the tracker goes off?" He smiled, pressed the start button, and then pointed at the ceiling.

"This whole shed's a Faraday cage. Keeps interference out, and radio in." I was impressed. The chicken wire on the roof was probably part of it. I checked my phone, and sure enough there was no signal.

"Come," said Marek, pulling his own phone out. "Let her warm up a bit," and he led me over to an old gramophone player, abandoned on a cardboard box serving as a low bench. On the turntable was an old 78, Bizet's *Carmen*, by Marek Weber and His Orchestra.

"You?" I joked.

"You noticed." He smiled, shaking his head, and moved the tone arm to activate the platter. As the haunting strains of the original bad romance crackled out, Marek stood up, pointed his phone at the spinning disk, and pressed a button. The phone screen showed the disk turning slower and slower until *His Master's Voice* was steady on the side of the screen, the logo inverted so that Nipper the dog looked like he was about to nose-dive into a funnel. Beside the still image appeared the speed: '79.4 RPM'. I was impressed and decided I needed to get an app that acted like a strobe—capable of freezing repetitive movement and determining rotational speed. Or at least get a phone that could load that app.

"So," said Marek as we went back over to the Veyron, "for 30 miles per hour, what rotational speed will we want?" He attached a bit of white tape to the wheel of the car to allow the strobe to work. The differing wheel sizes confused the calculation for a moment but we agreed that at 30 mph the tyre would revolve just over 371 times per minute.

Marek reached into the car and shifted the power to the front wheels. I leaned over and he showed me how to adjust the bracket, using his ear to judge the speed in third gear. To check, he got out, pointed his phone at the wheel until the white tape appeared stationary. 390.1 RPM. We judged it to be 31.5 mph.

"Now for the detector ..."

I thought Marek would fire up the HP but instead he picked up a CB walkie-talkie and turned the squelch down until it was silent.

"You know the noise your phone sometimes makes on the car radio?" I nodded. "Well, that's the noise the tracker makes. Which at least tells us it's using mobile phone signals to report its location."

We sat in silence for half an hour, listening to the purr of the engine. My ears felt like they were getting the aural equivalent of tunnel vision. Marek got up and killed the motor. "It would have triggered by now," he concluded.

"Maybe it needs a GPS signal, and in here," I shrugged, indicating the radio-blocking mesh that covered the walls and roof. He nodded, pleased that I was on the same page, and pointed to a little box, the size of a Wi-Fi access point, mounted at the apex of the barn's ceiling.

"GPS repeater. That's the transmitter. There's an antenna on the roof. When it's switched on, we can receive GPS in here. Same with Wi-Fi," he pointed to another box on the wall, "we can connect if we want to, but nothing gets out."

"Okay," I was trying hard to add some value to his knowledge, "so it's probably triggered by GPS movement, which we can't get in here. If the car isn't moving relative to the earth, it doesn't trigger."

"Yes," he said, "but I've tried putting it up on a flat bed and towing it, and that doesn't work."

"With the engine running?"

"With the engine running."

I was impressed by his thoroughness. "And what happens exactly when it does trigger?"

"Cops. Lots of cops. Probably private contractors pushing them. First time it happened was after we picked her up, up North; Manchester. Helena was driving. It was a Friday night, awful traffic, took us an hour just to get to the M6 so we were crawling.

"Going south, things cleared, so Helena opened up. Only doing 90, but suddenly we noticed the blue lights. Helena pulled over to the left lane while they were still a mile back. But it was us they were after."

"And they didn't pull you over, because? ..."

Marek smiled. "Because Helena let them sit behind her for a mile or so while we calculated our exit," he smiled, remembering, "and then she put her foot down and we took off. It was like they weren't even moving."

I smiled too, remembering her driving this morning.

"We hit the exit, dumped the car behind the services and walked for hours to get as far away as possible. Robert came to pick us up. You met Robert yet?" I shook my head.

"You will. We decided to risk driving back via the services and the car was still there. No cops. That got us thinking."

It got me thinking too. Alex, Marek, Robert. Certainly no shortage of men around her. I hastily refocused—I was missing the story.

"... an old Bedford horse box, covered all the openings with mesh to cage it, and we picked the car up a day later. I travelled all the way here in the back, trying to listen for the squawk, nothing. Worked it out from there."

"Maybe the cops were a fluke?" I wondered.

"Nah, we took it out a few times in the box after that. Smallish roads, easy to disappear. We went through the possibilities one by one:

"Left her sitting there. No attention.

"Started her up and left her for an hour. No attention. Drove for ten minutes. Nothing. Twenty minutes, nothing. Parked her back each time in the horsebox cage.

"Then we drove another twenty minutes, this time at speed. Then I heard the squawk," he patted the little radio. "Suddenly there's a helicopter. Luckily she was hidden away again and they criss-crossed overhead for half an hour before giving up.

"Tried it again, 40 miles away. This time we tried 40 minutes at 20 miles per hour, then 30 at 30 before she sang.

"We packed up and as we were heading home, we passed a couple of traffic cops, and a black Navara, steaming in the opposite direction."

I thought for a moment. "I don't suppose you can just sell it?" I asked.

"Well, part of Helena wants to. She thinks it's a crock. But she thinks it wouldn't be right to sell it until it's been neutralised.

"More than that, she'd like to get her hands on the joker who gave it to her as payment." To my enquiring look, he shook his head. "Long gone, but the real issue is, she really, really likes this baby."

We stared at the car. I shook my head. I couldn't think of anything that would help find the tracker. "So it must be related to GPS speed *and* wheel speed."

"I think so," he said, "the next step is probably a bigger covered van so I can put her on jacks, *and* get sufficient cooling, *and* get rid of the exhaust *and* not compromise the Faraday cage, to see if we can simulate all that."

"Well, I suppose it's do-able," I agreed. But was it worth it? It could be an expensive failure. We didn't need to say that to each other. As we stared at the car, I found myself liking this shared experience: this common ground.

"Well," Marek concluded, "it was worth asking."

"If I think of anything," I shrugged, and he thanked me.

We strolled down the length of the shed as he put things away. At the far end we turned into a passageway, and passed a room, lined with shelves all stacked with computers. I couldn't resist rubbernecking.

"Don't get excited," Marek laughed, "some of them are dead, some of them work, and most we just don't know. We've picked up a little collection here and there, some of them quite old, but Helena's very sentimental, she doesn't like the idea of scrapping them." He spoke of her with affection, but he didn't seem threatened by my presence.

Perhaps he didn't know she had brought me home last night. Or maybe he was just the handyman.

Peeping out from behind a display stand, I saw what I was looking for: an old laptop. I hauled it out. A Toshiba T5100 with both hard disk and floppy drive. I found a mains cable and looked triumphant.

Marek showed be where I could dust it off and wash my hands. The sink was next to a large office. The light was off but I recognised the digital printer; it occupied more floor length than the Bugatti and Golf combined. As I cleaned up, I pondered. Pigs; cars, no, cars with trackers; workshop; electronics; industrial printing. This was some enterprise Helena was running here. I wondered where the money came from. Marek's phone beeped.

"Oh, Helena's on her way back and said she'd meet you in her office for a cup of tea."

I dried my hands and then pointed to the office we had passed.

"No," he said, pointing to the main house, "inside." His eyes had followed mine to the open office door and I wondered if I had observed too much.

He was tensed as though to tackle me had I tried to enter the office. I wondered what I would have seen, and why he was suddenly looking very thoughtful. Not thoughtful, maybe angry, certainly very alert.

Marek might be compact, but he had picked up the 70 kg sack like it was nothing. I suddenly saw him for what he was, a very dangerous man, and with that recognition, I felt another twinge in the area of my stomach.

I had to get away. I excused myself from his gaze by remembering I had left my jacket and the floppies in the car. I rolled down my sleeves and clutching the laptop walked carefully back the way I had come, trying hard not to stare at anything.

I felt like his eyes were on my back even after I had turned the corner. I put on the jacket and, just to be safe, I decided to enter the house from the front, in case he was still waiting round the back.

9 – A Study of Devastation

I opened the front door without knocking, but carefully, still ill at ease from my encounter with Marek.

No crossbow bolts thudded theatrically into the floor around me.

I shut the door, with a definite clunk to announce my presence, and entered the main hall. The lounge door was shut, but the dining room open, so I peeked inside.

In the middle on the far side of the table sat a middle-aged man, staring absent-mindedly at a laptop in front of him. His head was raised to peer through the bottom of his glasses, with his thumb propping up his chin, and forefinger stroking his cheek.

The pose was reminiscent of a classical seer, and the flecks of grey at his temples reinforced the image. He reminded me of a serious newsreader, or the kind who would narrate nature documentaries. He looked up as I entered, but didn't seem surprised to see me.

"Ah," he said, "you must be James. Excuse me not getting up."

He didn't say why. I nodded and managed a 'Hi'.

"I'm Robert Banks, and Cat has been telling me all about you." The emphasis on the word *all* made me anxious. "Do sit down."

I started moving to sit opposite him, but he waved me to the head of the table, from where I would have a view into the garden. I placed the laptop and bag of floppies on the table.

"So," he said as I sat, "how did you get on this morning?"

I wondered if I should be telling him about Helena's business and he must have sensed the reason for my hesitation because he smiled kindly and said, "Oh, don't worry. I'm Helena's solicitor, and her financial adviser. I live here, more or less, so you can tell me everything."

Again the emphasis, this time on the last word. Whereas

Marek's compact strength had worried me, it was not Robert's size that was of concern, but rather the way he appeared to effortlessly dissect me with his words while exuding warmth and congeniality.

I gave him a potted overview of the trip to town. He nodded and questioned occasionally, not missing details, and made me go back a few times to cover things I had left out. It felt as though he had already read the entire script and was testing me on it.

I realised quickly that his greying head was not an indicator of senility, and Robert should not be underestimated. He asked me a bit about my family, my past, my jobs, and again, there were little details that suggested he was probing, while his bonhomie and intelligence meant I found myself enjoying the process.

I'll admit, my CV is a little overstated. I have found it helpful in getting work, but very quickly I saw the futility of trying to put something across this sharp-witted man, and so I told him the simple truth. I wondered if he didn't know it already.

The interview ended when he gave a long satisfied sigh, arching his back. "I think you'll find Helena's ready for you. Turn left, then first right and follow your nose." He motioned me to the door.

I got up, about to shake hands, but he smiled and looked down at his laptop. I took my dismissal and went looking for Helena's study.

***

I didn't mean to be subversive, but nature called, and so I didn't follow Robert's directions to the letter. After a little exploration I found a relaxingly spacious convenience in a room not far from the kitchen. I locked the door and sat down to give myself time to think.

Both Robert and Marek had seemed benign enough on the surface. But Marek's sudden change from good humour to intense caution had disturbed me. And then Robert's outwardly friendly but precise cross-examination had left me feeling exposed and out of place. I felt very inadequate.

All in all, there were some very capable men working with Helena. Marek; Robert; and the as-yet unseen Alex.

I might be good at technology, but my skills didn't match up to what I had seen here so far. It wasn't in my nature to fight hard to impress a girl. I found it improbable that Helena would find me interesting on a personal level.

I could only assume that this was, in fact, just a job, and I felt somewhat betrayed that she had implied that there might have been more. I tried hard to remember her exact words of last night, but with all the excitement of the day, my thinking was somewhat unclear.

Certainly my interest was piqued. As jobs went, this was a pretty good number even though the cast seemed quite intimidating. I hoped on a good day I could hold my own; however my confidence was starting to wane.

With a start I realised I had taken a bit too long with this little mulling session, and even though I was not any closer to understanding my feelings, I had to press on and I knew it was time to make a decision or two.

I was no good at chat-up lines, but maybe Helena needed me to declare my interest.

Now or never, I said to myself. I opened the door and left the bathroom.

I followed the paintings that led me in the direction Robert had indicated down a corridor lined with a dark wood.

I squared my shoulders and determined to be bold. Several doors led off the passageway, all unmarked. I had no difficulty in finding Helena's study because as I turned the corner, I saw Marek leaving it. My shoulders were suddenly anything but squared.

I was still uneasy from my earlier meeting with him, but it was not the sight of him in the doorway that made my feelings sink; rather it was the farewell kiss Helena was giving him. I lost hope completely.

It was a short kiss, but passionate, and full on the lips, and their eyes and faces smiled as they gazed at each other afterwards.

Not just the handyman, then. My heart crashed through the floor.

They hadn't seen me, and I managed to reverse out of sight. I hung back as they exchanged a few last murmured words. The door closed and I waited a moment before rounding the corner again, smiling brightly, fully expecting to bump into him. Thankfully, he must have gone the other way.

I stopped, and took a moment to try to still my thoughts. This was more like the life I knew. I was a fool to think a girl like Helena would think of me as anything other than a hired hand. With a deep sigh, I knocked.

"Come in."

The simple words re-awoke conflicting emotions inside. I opened the door, and found myself transported a hundred years or more into the past.

The study was a beautiful space. Manly, but with little touches that spoke of other interests: the panelled walls with old prints. Red and yellow tulips in a modern glass vase on the side table. It was a bit late for tulips, so these probably weren't cheap. I could imagine an old master in this very room, painting them.

The rich walnut desk, with its little doors on either side facing the sittee, not the sitter. The Lagavulin single malt in the cabinet behind her, a bottle of Baileys on the mantlepiece beside two squat, fluted shot glasses. The lighting dim, and tungsten, casting its warming glow. A coal fire murmuring contentedly to itself in the hearth. I fell in love, all over again. This time with the place, and it broke my heart to think I would never see it again.

"Come in," she repeated, as I hung by the doorway taking

it all in. I looked at her, and she was smiling. A new stab of pain intensified the weakness in my knees.

I remembered last night. Just last night! I could hardly compass the various feelings that I had experienced since our meeting in the bus shelter.

"Sit down, James." I gladly sank into the chair. At least I no longer needed to control my knees.

Helena got up and walked round the desk to shut the door. I felt bad she had to do it, but on the plus side, I noticed that her red trousers had been replaced by a similar coloured crepe skirt, with grey tights sculpting her legs, which ended in short little boots. I enjoyed the look until I remembered that she wasn't mine to enjoy.

I looked up again quickly and met those eyes with their knowing smile. Speech deserted me, and I wondered if I would ever be able to form a coherent sentence around her, even if I were to meet her every day for a year. She was truly devastating.

"Tea?"

I nodded dumbly, and she poured, moved my cup closer and passed me the little silver cake platter of petits fours. I shook my head. They looked delicious, but my stomach felt like a rat was remodelling its lodgings within.

She reached down into a drawer by her side and drew out an unsealed envelope, placing it before me before sitting down.

"Thank you," she said, as I reached for it.

It was fifties. I didn't bother to count it, but tucked it into my jacket. No, her jacket; the jacket she had bought me.

"And you can keep the suit."

I tried to look grateful but thoughts of Marek stole my smile. I could see that my manner was puzzling her. I didn't want to be a jerk.

"Thank you." I managed to rescue my expression with a wry grimace.

"Marek says you were most helpful."

"I wasn't that useful." I took a sip of tea to try to calm my heaving insides, but this just made it worse. I put the cup down. I had the money. Now I wanted to run—I realised I was tense.

She frowned. Clearly I was managing to be a jerk without trying too hard.

"He said you figured out the simple stuff straight away and you noticed lots of details, the record label, the sack, the printer."

I shrugged.

"And you offered to think about the problem, even though you knew you were leaving today, so that means you thought you might have a better idea before knocking-off time?"

Well, that was true. My thoughts returned to the car, and while the technical part of my brain was absorbed in the Bugatti problem, what was on the top of my mind just spilled out.

"I saw!"

I was shocked I had said it aloud. I hadn't meant to speak, but once I realised what I was saying, I tried to sound angry. Instead, the words came out with a sob, my hand waving wildly at the door.

Helena looked perplexed for a moment until the realisation dawned of what I had seen. She looked stricken, putting her hand to her face. I had to look away.

"Marek? Oh, James. I'm so sorry."

She searched for words.

"It's not like that. It's ... it's ... complicated." She sighed in frustration.

I dared to look back, but that was a mistake. Her face was so forlorn that every piece of my White Knight DNA wanted to muscle in and rescue her. Mr Grumpy assured me he was not going to let that happen.

And, thankfully, it was he who saved me from an early

departure.

I recognised his old familiar voice, and realised then that I hadn't heard from him nor his henchmen all afternoon. Not since after lunch. They had been silent the entire time I was searching the skip, and driving the wreck, and playing investigator in the garage. Even while I had been mulling in the ablutions, they had been silent. And it had been fine. No, not fine, it had been wonderful. The whole day had been marvellous.

I didn't want Mr Grumpy. I wanted Helena, and if I couldn't have her, then I would be content merely to be her rescuer. To rescue her from jerks. Jerks like me. I slumped, simultaneously trapped and defeated.

"James. Please. Please can you give me some time?" She was trying to sort things out, I could see that. My despair must have been plain. She was on her knees in front of my chair, holding my hand in hers. I didn't remember her moving there.

"Please," she begged again, "promise me"—her voice firmed—"James, promise me two things."

I looked at her, my heart breaking to see her so close with a chasm so wide between us. I breathed deeply and she took this as a positive sign.

"I need your help."

I sat there, trying merely to look at her. Trying not to *gaze*. Her request for help ensnaring me most effectively.

"Look, I understand if you just want to leave. But could you give me a few days?" I looked uncertain. "Well, at least until tomorrow?"

Mr Grumpy and Co were obviously off somewhere licking their wounds since no retort sprang to mind. She seized the opportunity.

"Stay a few days, help me with this case, please."

Case? What kind of case? Perhaps without knowing it, she had appealed to my analytical side. There were so many questions, and what could I do? So much was unanswered and I wasn't sure my emotions could take any more pleading. I nodded my agreement.

She sprang up, her mind clearly involved in complex calculations. It was quite disconcerting how fast I seemed to vanish from right in front of her. I stood up too, angling for a bit more attention.

She turned towards the door, one finger held up to stay me, her eyes locked onto mine.

"Wait here. I just have to tell Cleo you're staying for dinner —" and she disappeared down the corridor.

I believed the 'just have to tell Cleo' part. It was the slight hesitation before the word 'staying' that I was not convinced by, as though she had been about to say something else.

I stared at the empty doorway, wondering if I had betrayed my very self by giving in so easily.

I felt Mr Grumpy rising to his feet to make a well-aimed accusation. I felt him look around the room surveying his audience of doppelgängers, calculating the timing of his delivery to perfection. He took a deep breath to start his exposition, and then he evaporated as the empty doorway failed to remain empty.

"I forgot something," she said, breathless, not slowing down until she collided with me.

I staggered back into the desk, half-sitting on its edge, and then she was between my legs, her arms wrapped round my neck, her lips on mine, and she was kissing me, a wild, passionate, abandoned kiss.

'Much longer than with Marek,' Mr Logical informed me, but before I could respond to him, she broke off and ran back to the door, looking back at me over her shoulder, her eyes so delighted that I felt my whole heart sing. Then she was gone.

I lowered myself, letting the desk take my full weight. My heart might be floating, but the rest of my body needed some support.

'That girl is trouble—' Nan was flanked by Mr Grumpy and Mr Logical.

"Nan," I said to the empty room, "you've said that before. And anyway, *you* weren't invited to stay." I turned my back on them.

***

I waited fifteen minutes in her study, and in the end it wasn't Helena who returned, but one of the twins carrying a small bag. Pink plimsolls.

"Cat?" I ventured.

"Well done," she smiled, almost shyly. It was very fetching. "Um, Helena says sorry, but she's still in a meeting. She also said you'll be working here for a few days."

I nodded. She put down her bag.

"So, we have a very strict health and drugs policy—" the elf looked right at me. "Are you drug and disease free?" A little smile cushioned her directness. I nodded, slightly taken aback.

"Would you mind us checking?" She reached into the medical bag and took out a syringe.

Imposition aside, it seemed quite a lot of checking for a few days' work, and by the time the results came back I would be gone. But I didn't feel like arguing. Emotionally I was drained. Indeed, I was in no position to argue—it was their workplace after all. Her house, her rules.

"Shall I sit?" I pointed at the chair.

"Here's fine," she said, and suddenly she too was standing between my legs, wrapping the band of the pressure cuff around my arm, and pumping it up. She wasn't shy to make contact, leaning back into me.

She moved only to insert the needle and take three short tubes of blood. I looked away while she did it. I didn't mind the jab of the needle; it was the sight of it that got me.

She put the bloods in an envelope, the rubbish in the bin, and everything else back in the bag. Finally she stuck a small piece of cotton wool on my forearm with a plaster. And then she leaned over the spot and kissed it better. I hadn't ever read about *that* in the workplace guide.

"Helena asked if you would you like to take a shower and have an explore, dinner is only at eight—" and she was gone.

I sank back into the chair and decided to finish my cup of tea.

10 – Dinner Democracy

After I had managed a couple of the cakes, I looked around the ground floor. I was hoping for a bit of company, but the house seemed deserted. Even the kitchen was empty, although something smelled good in there. Roast beef, my nose decided.

I collected the old laptop and floppies from the dining table and found my way back to my room.

I kicked off my shoes, and as I hung up my suit, I felt the biohazard pen-meter in my pocket. I took it out and placed it on the bedside table.

The little desk had power and a comfortable chair. I plugged the laptop in and was delighted as it whirred to life. The disks were easy enough to read, and each contained a single small file named 'Sales Data' followed by a date. I couldn't open the files themselves which were more modern that the ancient DOS would allow. I used the debug program to look at the contents, but found nothing suspicious on the parts of the text that were decipherable. Surely this wasn't enough sales data for a company the size of Pharmaply?

The sugar low after the cakes was beginning to kick in. I had meant to take a shower, but decided to rest my eyes for a few moments on the bed instead.

***

I could feel her hands on my shoulders kissing me, her voice laughing, saying "James, James," and as I came to, I reached up and pulled her down on top of me. She landed sprawling and I enjoyed her weight on top of me.

I opened my eyes and found myself face to face with a business-like matron who looked a little shocked.

"James!" she repeated. She stopped shaking my shoulder. Apparently I had imagined the kissing bit. I removed my hand from her back and she spryly jumped off the bed, her grubby jodhpurs leaving a smudge on the cover. I looked at it, and at her, and felt very guilty.

"Sorry." I tried to find a suitable excuse for accosting her. She smiled forgiveness, even as she tried rubbing the bedcover to remove the mark.

"Cat will kill me," she muttered.

"I'm sorry," I repeated, and she straightened, put out her hand to pull me up, and then shook it.

"Hi, I'm Alex."

I'm afraid that I stared.

"Oh, I'm sorry. I thought you were a boy. I mean, a man."

"No need to get personal—" the smile again allayed any offence. "I can assure you, I am entirely woman." I could see that, and she made a couple of adjustments to emphasise the fact, before continuing.

"I was sent to find you, everyone's already downstairs. I'm late in because I had to jab Hamlet, so, you and I need to get changed, pronto!"

She headed for the door, turned back and pointed at a dinner jacket ensemble lying on the bed. It hadn't been there earlier.

"You've got ten minutes. The shower's running. Mush," she clapped her hands and shut the door behind her. I doubted that ten minutes would be enough, but I hated being late, and so after a rather rushed shower, I was ready. On the way downstairs, I caught my reflection in the mirror on the landing. It was a very flattering impression, but I had no time to stop and stare.

***

Luckily, my fear of being the last to arrive was groundless. Only Robert and Marek were in the living room as I entered, and we shook hands in a very formal way.

Robert studied me. He pointed at my tie, held up his finger to indicate he knew the solution, and crossed to the door.

"Cat," he called, and a few moments later she appeared, in a flouncy pink number with satin shoes. I bent down a little and she deftly twisted the bow into shape, smoothed down my collar, and gave me a little peck on the cheek. She vanished again as I thanked her.

Robert offered me a drink and I accepted a small beer. Marek was drinking his out of the bottle, so I chose to join him. Robert had chosen a glass of red wine. He was clearly at ease and happy to carry the conversation. He told an improbable story about a client which I thought might be apocryphal, but it broke the ice and I smiled and raised my drink in appreciation.

As we clinked, Helena entered. We were not talking at the time, yet the room stilled as we surveyed the girl in the simple tunic dress of turquoise lace, held up by a single swathe of fabric over her left shoulder. Mesh panels on the bias gave the impression the bodice had been draped over her. Her short red bob was beautifully offset by the gown. She stood there, her head slightly tilted, happily absorbing the effect she had created.

Robert recovered first, and strode over to take her hand to his lips.

"My dear, how ravishing you look." Helena preened and twirled once. Her entrance complete, she got right to business.

"Where is everyone? Come on, let's go in, and if they're late they can starve." We started to move but she gestured at Marek and me. "No bottles at the table." She left, with Robert in her wake.

Marek looked at me with his eyebrows raised attempting to appear long-suffering. I just smiled. We tipped the bottles high and swallowed the rest of our beers before following.

In the hall we met Alex, who was just going in. I was getting used to the idea of fancy frocks, but her red satin dress, backed with a multitude of thin crossed straps, provided a subtle moulding to her lovely figure. I let her go ahead of me. It was the polite thing to do, I told myself, as I admired her back.

The same room as breakfast was now a fairy tale of elegance. The table had been shortened to allow for more intimate conversation. It was covered in a white tablecloth and set for eight, with three tall candlesticks providing the light. Helena was standing at the garden side, the gold curtains offsetting her dress wonderfully. She directed Marek to her left, and Robert to her right.

"James, would you be a dear, and look after the girls at that end of the table?" She caught me staring at Alex again, and she tilted her head in feigned warning at my guilty look, while pointing to the end chair opposite hers. I nodded. "Alex, you're next to James on his left." Now I wasn't sure the warning was feigned. I tried to look serious, and held Alex's chair for her. Helena sat too, and we men next.

Cat entered carrying soup plates. Behind her was the girl Helena had apologised to outside the garage earlier. Her name was Celestine, I recalled, as I watched her carry in a large wooden board of steaming baguettes. I caught the smell of freshly baked bread as Helena directed her to the space between Robert and Alex, leaving the two chairs nearest the door for the twins. Cat plonked herself down next to Marek and gave him a big hug. Helena sent her to sit next to me. She pouted, but moved. Marek laughed, which elicited a bigger pout.

Cleo entered, carrying a tureen. She placed it centre-stage, removed the lid, and then sat next to Marek. Unlike her sister's pink dress, her dress was less fussy, a steely grey close-fitting creation that reached to her knees. She too leaned into Marek, and gave him a hug. I wondered if I should feel left out. Helena got up to serve, realised the reach was a bit much for her, and delegated the job to Cleo. I licked my lips as the smell of fresh basil and sage drifted over the table.

"Cook *and* serve," Cleo muttered good-naturedly as she ladled the rich tomato soup into the plates before passing them down the table. Robert took the opportunity to pour wine, an aromatic white. Cleo sat, and Helena raised her glass.

"To working together—" We echoed her toast, and drank.

I started my soup. Delicious.

For the next few minutes I used the silence to study Celestine surreptitiously. She wore a black dress with a brocade corset top. Iridescent red and green peeked through, playing tricks on the eye. I could just see a matching bow in the broad plait of her raven hair—a very Celtic princess.

'Perhaps Oriental?' suggested Mr Logical.

I looked again, and noticed her eyes were brown and slightly turned up at the outside edges. Earlier, I had assumed her brows were arched by emotion but they were just following the natural curves of her face. Perhaps she had accentuated them, but when viewed head on they looked like beautifully crafted gull-wings. Her lips were generous and full, and then I saw that her top lip echoed the gull motive. Hers was a very interesting face, I thought.

Celestine looked up, caught me staring, and scowled. I could see she was much younger than I, and when she frowned, I recalled the argument of earlier in the day.

The others seemed very comfortable in each other's company. Much of the conversation was gentle ribbing about foibles of the recent past. Robert walked round the table again, topping up the wine. He asked my opinion of it and I admitted that while I liked it, I didn't really know much about wines. Robert winked and showed me the label. "This is a Pinot Noir, Blaauwklippen," he explained. "Not one of their older red vintages, of course, just a little something made for friends. Lovely nose, very fragrant, easy to drink. Doesn't compete too much with the soup." He moved on, to top up Cat's glass.

"Yes," said Helena, "one shouldn't really have wine with soup." I looked up and realised this was another tease.

Robert bowed deferentially, but gave as good as he got, affecting a slight accent. "The lady is indeed correct, young master. Yes sir." He paused, getting the timing right. "If you stay a few days the Mistress will acquaint you with *many* aspects of wine."

Helena snorted indignantly, while everyone else laughed, including Cat who had just taken a sip. The resulting spluttering caused more hilarity, and even Celestine couldn't help herself, and smiled.

I looked round the table. It felt good to be there.

I finished my soup, mopping up the final drops with a chunk of the warm baguette. Cat and Cleo got up to clear the plates, and let me carry the remainder of the bread out. I expected to help carry something back, but instead I was shooed back to the table. Cat returned to take out the tureen, and the mood became more serious.

"Celestine," Helena asked, "do you have the book?" The girl reached under the table for a bag, and extracted a textbook-sized paperback from it. She passed it silently to Alex who then gave it to me.

The distinctive black and yellow cover proclaimed 'Industrial Espionage for Dummies'. The cover featured a girl in a balaclava looking very Bond-like. At the bottom left, in bold letters, was the author's name: *Helena Fey.*

Everyone seemed to be holding their breath, judging my reaction. So, they were spies. Not MI5-type spies, but commercial spies. Stealing secrets for money. Mr Grumpy got in first: 'I knew it!' Mr Logical hastened to point out that spying on one's competitors wasn't necessarily illegal.

I kept my eyes firmly on the cover while I tried to decide what I thought. I could feel the whole table looking at me. I remembered the lighter mood of a few moments ago. A quick idea sprang to mind, and I said, "*You* wrote a book?"

Everyone laughed, and the tension dissipated. Helena tried to look injured but it was difficult for her to do so while smiling.

Cleo explained. "No, it's a joke, a dummy book, get it?" I looked inside, and indeed the first few pages had been blank but were now inscribed with birthday wishes to Helena from the ensemble. A little further on was a Dilbert annual, rebound as part of the book to give it bulk. I closed it, and nodded.

"We gave it to Helena for her thirtieth," said Cleo, and realising this might have been indiscreet information, she tried to make amends by adding "Last month." Cat stepped in to help her stop digging, taking the book from me and pointing at the title.

"Had you guessed?" she asked.

"No," I admitted, "although I think I would have got there in a little while."

'You might have got there sooner if you weren't being distracted by all these girls,' Mr Logical pointed out, managing to sound a little offended.

"So, this is how you earn a living?" I directed this at Helena.

"Okay," she said looking round, "cards on the table?" Everyone nodded and looked expectant. I sat back.

"James, my clients come to me for information about their competitors. I acquire that information for them. Happy to discuss the ethics sometime, but it usually involves rooting around in skips. And, today, you proved you can do that."

Everyone smiled, and I remembered the meter I had brought down to give back to her. "Oh, I've got your biohazard thingy here." I held it up.

I didn't get the reaction I was expecting.

Silence fell around the table, and everyone looked puzzled except Helena who had stopped mid-flow with her mouth slightly open. A moment later, while Marek and Robert were still frowning at it, several gasps suggested the girls had recognised it. Helena now looked a bit guilty. Celestine burst into tears. I looked at the pen and then at them. Cat reached over and gently took it out of my hand.

"It isn't a biohazard meter," she whispered, "it's a fertility test." She looked at the smiley face and added, "Used." I looked to Helena for an explanation, but so was everyone else.

"All right, all right," she tried to restore calm. "I *found* it. Under the table at breakfast, all right?" From the sob that came from Celestine, we all guessed who had dropped it. "We do need to talk about this," she surveyed them, "but not here, not now." Robert nodded. Alex had her arm around the bowed Celestine. "Right now, we need to talk about Pharmaply."

"But first," she stood. "Robert, may we start on the red, please? And, Celestine, please could we step out for a minute?" Robert got up, and Alex helped Celestine to the door. Helena waved her away, and took the girl out with her.

For the eight minutes that they were gone, we sat in silence, taking occasional sips of the heavy wine. It struck me that it wasn't an uncomfortable silence, more a solemn standing together in solidarity. I felt warmth and empathy and deep companionship, emphasised by the wordless expression of ... I searched for the word, and the only one which would come was *love*. This was love, and I felt my spine quiver as I realised how much I wanted to belong. They seemed to belong together, and I wondered if I could ever belong anywhere like this.

Cleo stuck her head into Marek's chest and said, "We should get the food in."

He, Cleo and Cat trooped out and were bringing back the first of the dishes when Helena returned, her arm around the slightly happier looking Celestine. Helena led her round the back, past Robert, and then said, "Budge over, Robert, there's a good chap." He did so happily, leaving Helena to install Celestine next to herself.

"Sorry," the still red-eyed girl said to the table.

“Nothing to forgive,” said Cleo as she passed by, giving the girl a kiss on the cheek. Cat repeated this on the other cheek, and Marek gave her a hug before he sat down. Alex blew her a kiss and one of her infectious smiles that even Celestine couldn’t resist.

“Absolutely,” said Robert, “nothing to forgive, old girl,” and he stretched his arm around her, pulling her into himself. She snuggled there while Helena carved the magnificent looking beef, still on the rib, its thick crust of caramelised fat glistening in the candlelight.

The heady smell from the oven earlier wafted over the table, tickling my appetite. The dishes spread around held roast potatoes, carrots, parsnips, and what I thought was swede but turned out to be butternut squash. On the sideboard, waiting for room, were cabbage and Yorkshire puddings.

The dishes were quickly passed and plates filled, with much good-natured jostling for vegetables, horseradish and gravy. I put a large spoon of French mustard on my plate, and, taking my cue from Helena, tucked in. The cabbage turned out to be dressed with milk and nutmeg which both softened the taste and added a spicy tang to the bouquet.

***

I know we managed two bottles of the white wine, but I don’t recall how many of the red Robert poured out, glass by glass. I wasn’t drunk, but I was very, very happy as the main course wound down. Cat and Cleo squabbled over a titbit from the carving board—only to have Marek steal it at the last moment.

Helena had kept Celestine close, comforting her. She even fed the girl little morsels from her plate, nudging her, teasing her, to make her smile, and they stared into each other’s eyes like young lovers, sharing a joke.

Robert, meanwhile, looking replete, sat back in his chair, gazing at the rest of us, a look of contentment settling over him.

It was Alex who got up to answer the phone. She came back a few seconds later and whispered in Helena's ear. Helena looked thoughtful, then pleased, and planted a final kiss on Celestine's forehead. She straightened up in her chair, and banged her spoon on the table.

"I think we are going to have to do most of this business tomorrow. However, as you all know, as part of our agreement we publish all test results." She looked around to make sure everyone was paying full attention.

"Robert and Alex, yours are back and you're all good." That didn't seem to surprise anybody. "James," she looked straight at me in that disconcerting way, "your earlies are back and they're all good. More to come." She smiled, and paused before continuing.

"Now, you know that I've asked James to stay and work with us for a while." Everyone nodded. "Well, before dessert then, that just leaves the ballot. As you know, I have proposed James work with us on probation, and everyone gets a vote. Not you, James, sorry." The wine had relaxed me, but even so, I couldn't look at the girl's dancing eyes without it triggering a thrill of excitement. She started on her left, "Marek?"

He nodded, and said a quiet yes.

"Cleo?"

"Oh, yes."

"Cat?"

"Definitely." And I got a kiss.

"Alex?"

"Most definitely." I got another kiss.

"Robert?"

"Yes, indeed. Wonderful idea."

"Celestine?"

The girl's eyes were wet again, but she nodded her head in assent, convincing herself.

"And me. I vote yes." Helena finished, and got a laugh.

Crème brûlée were served in individual ramekins and consumed with pleasure, each break of the golden sugar crust releasing a trace of vanilla and lime, the smooth custard gliding down the tongue. Finally, we moved back to the lounge. The *drawing* room, Helena called it.

Helena called us to order.

"Maybe we should introduce ourselves so James knows how we all fit in?" I thought I had a fair idea, but it would be good to get the details.

Marek started. "Hello, James, I'm Marek." Helena glared at him and he dropped the affected formal tone. "I look after the mechanical stuff."

"And?" prompted Helena.

"And cars and things."

"Hopeless." Helena shook her head, clearly proud of her crew. She decided to take over. "Marek looks after the cars, the workshop and garage, and the house. He also handles plumbing, electrics, networking, computing, and printing. And anything else that needs handling." Cleo giggled, and she too got a sharp look from her boss.

Helena pointed with her nose. "And that's Cleo, superb cook, and in charge of the kitchen, and helps Cat with the house. Cat, who does the household stuff such as laundry and helps Cleo with the cooking. They also do odd jobs." Helena skipped me and waved a hand towards at Alex. "Alex is quartermaster and looks after the grounds; the livestock; and the workers who don't live in." Alex inclined her head in acknowledgement.

"Robert, dear friend, financial wizard and lawyer *par excellence*. Just don't play cards with him," which got a laugh from Marek.

"And last, and if sometimes last in line, then still first in our hearts, the very much-loved Celestine, loved more than she can imagine, who handles the admin, the bills and who you met earlier on the phone as the voice of the Pharma

Inspectorate." My eyes widened. Celestine looked pleased at the introduction.

There was some cheese with biscuits on the side table, and Robert handed out port. My new colleagues patted me on the back, kissed and hugged me, and offered me their congratulations. Helena did not. She stood over by the windows, surveying her crew, looking happy, and smoking a cigar. Robert stole a puff or two from her.

With a raise of her eyes, and a slight tilt of the rolled leaf, she offered me a puff, but I declined.

It was the strangest, but probably the best job interview I had ever had.

11 – Après Dinner

Half an hour later, things in the drawing room wound down a bit. Their port glasses drained, Marek excused himself and left. Cleo followed soon after.

Robert had put out a card table and was shuffling the decks, Cat sitting on his right. Alex hesitated, about to excuse herself, but on seeing Celestine, decided to stay, and they completed the foursome. Helena gave them all pecks on the cheek, and stretched out her hand to me.

"Come on, Mr Glass, I think you need an early night."

I thought so too. The clock striking on the mantelpiece told me we had met almost exactly twenty-four hours ago. My stomach reminded me that I was still on very uncertain ground.

Helena, however, took my hand and, once out of earshot of the card players, whispered softly as we walked, "You alright?" I just nodded, tense. "Don't worry, it'll be fine, okay?" I nodded again, sure that her expectation was probably higher than the likely reality. She looked at me and took me by the waist, giving me a little tug, and repeated in a mock serious tone, complete with eyebrows, "Don't worry, I won't let you go." We both laughed at her stalker impression.

We walked upstairs slowly, which, given the wine, was probably a good idea, but it also meant lots of opportunity to hold on to each other, which was quite good fun. The rippling shoulders that I had seen that morning felt firm under my hand. Whatever she did, she didn't just sit around looking pretty.

She led me up the back stairs—I recognised them from last night. We passed by my room and she opened the door to the next one.

"This is me," she said, pulling me in and then letting go so I could look around.

It was almost identical to mine, except one wall was

accented with a deep turquoise that resonated with her dress.

She moved to the windows and closed the heavy drapes. I judged the door off to the right led to the bathroom shared with my room.

I turned back and saw her standing there, her hands behind her back, swaying shyly, and I took a whole new meaning from the words she had just murmured—'this is me'. It *was* her. Bold, in charge, definite, no-nonsense Helena. But also peeping through, just as I had seen last night at the bus shelter, was the younger, more vulnerable Helena. The one I wanted to hold and to protect.

"James—" She crossed the room, and took both my hands in hers, facing me, looking straight at me, her eyes wide, the green mesmerising; mine searing under the directness of her gaze "—you need to understand something."

I nodded, trying not to look alarmed. "This is going to happen, James, if you want." She inclined her head to indicate the bed. I wasn't sure if a nod was the right thing, and Mr Grumpy et al. seemed to have chosen the early bedtime option, abandoning me. So I was on my own, looking at her, worried about where she was going with this.

"But," she bit the side of her lip, "you have to know that no matter where this goes, I can't be *just* yours. This can't be an exclusive thing. There are ... others." Now I nodded. "That's it, that's all." She was looking at me as though I might bite.

I felt deep relief. I had already figured out that a girl like this would have a boyfriend, maybe even plenty of them. I assumed there must be others elsewhere, but I wondered about those living here. 'Never mix business with pleasure' is what Mr Grumpy would have said if he was awake. I wondered if Marek was one of them, but his going off with Cleo had been a bit obvious even though they had tried to disguise it by leaving separately. I smiled and decided to discount what I had seen earlier outside her study.

"I understand," I nodded to show that I did, "and it's fine.

I'm fine with that."

She looked a bit more certain, and asked me to undo the back of her dress. It appeared she was minimising on laundry bills as far as any other clothing was concerned. It took me a bit longer to shed my outfit, and then we had a shower.

Later there were a short few minutes of wonder. But she kept hold of my hand as she had promised, and let her tongue do most of the talking and in no time she had reacquired the response she desired. This time I felt we covered some ground before things went misty again.

12 – The Breakfast Club

I awoke to see Helena opening the curtains. Another bright day.

She smiled and crossed to the bedside table which sported a tray bearing two steaming mugs. As she handed me one, I had a sense of déjà vu, except that this time she hadn't bothered with the vest or the joggers.

We sat together and sipped hot tea. I enjoyed being there together, and idly wondered if hot drinks had been invented just to slow people down.

A little later we found out the convenience of having both his and hers toilets in the bathroom. During this, she showed me how to do Kegel exercises.

"Muscle tone is very important," she informed me, as we returned to the bedroom. She took her own advice seriously and, despite being in a hurry to get down for breakfast, she made me help her with her exercises while she sat astride me reading the news on her iPad. She only allowed me to finish after some minutes. She looked pleased, so I felt pleased too.

I needed to get my suit and a clean shirt and so she let me go with a kiss and a promise to see her at breakfast.

"James, I'm glad you stayed," she murmured.

I was glad too.

***

I took the back stairs down—my geography of the house was improving—and I found myself arriving in good time with the others in the dining room.

Over tea and toast, Helena banged her spoon and started.

"For the benefit of James, I'll fill in a few details the rest of you already know. But there's also some new stuff to discuss."

Helena took a mouthful, and waved her knife around. "It's probably best if I start at the beginning," she said.

Helena took a breath. I almost expected her to start with 'Once upon a time'.

"Pharmaply, who we visited yesterday, are a pharmaceutical company who developed a number of good drugs in the nineties." She looked round to make sure everyone was on the same page. I nodded, to say I was.

"However, the patents on those drugs are coming to an end. Pharmaply have announced they are developing new drugs, but nothing about what these are, or even the therapeutic area they are in."

This much I understood easily. Pharma companies are always trying for new drugs, but they take years to bring to market.

"Zolotran are another pharmaceutical company that are looking to invest in new drugs. They are interested in acquiring Pharmaply, but they want to know what Pharmaply are developing. So they asked me, Helena Fey, industrial spy, to find out."

I looked up, and she acknowledged the interruption. "How do they get hold of you," I asked, "do you advertise?"

Helena smiled.

"Well, yes, but not openly. Industrial espionage is big business, but no one likes to admit they are using it. We have drop boxes and indirect means to get in contact, and we rely on discretion to avoid being outed. A lot of the business is word of mouth."

"And disguises," I added, thinking of the wigs and clothes.

"Well, yes, some. Mostly whatever is appropriate for blending in."

"You wore a miniskirt to blend in while breaking into a pharma company?" This had been bugging me.

"No, silly, the clothing was for the nightclub."

I was puzzled. It wasn't so much because of how nightclubs had unexpectedly entered the conversation as the fact that Helena was looking a bit embarrassed. My confusion left a silence which she saw the need to fill.

"There's a nightclub in one of the units near Pharmaply.

I'd been stringing along one of the guys who works on their loading bay. That night he texted me and we met up at the club for a bit, before I persuaded him to show me around his wonderful workplace."

I could feel a slight awkwardness around me. Celestine was watching the table closely. It would be a good time to change the subject.

"Not a bad disguise," I said hurriedly, trying, but failing, to lighten the mood.

Helena, however, was more successful with her parry. "By the way, that tattoo you were trying to save came off in the shower last night." This got a laugh, breaking the tension. I felt embarrassed at the revelation, but most of the others were smiling good-naturedly. Helena took advantage of this to get back on track.

"So, our contact at Zolotran is a guy called Street. He asked me to find out what they were up to. I had a good nose around at Pharmaply"—she smiled—"the night we met, but found very little. The only unusual thing were those old floppy diskettes which I picked up. I was still having a look around when I tripped some alarm. In case I got caught, I dumped the stuff in the skip, where you retrieved it from, and ran." She paused, and I nodded again. It all seemed straightforward enough. "The problem was, they had guns."

"Guns?" Cleo voice echoed concern. I noticed that neither Marek nor Robert looked surprised—they had heard this before.

"Yes, with silencers. I heard three shots ricochet near me. I was running so hard I fell and grazed my knee. And my phone." I remembered the knee.

"I phoned Mr Xander Street and asked him what was going on but he told me it was my own fault. I got the impression he expected guns. Bastard. I didn't tell him I took the disks, because I didn't know if I could get them out of the skip. Besides, my phone chose that moment to die."

I remembered her sob. Knowing a bit more about her now, I realised it was probably frustration with her phone, rather than tears. However, the thought that someone had been shooting at her re-ignited all the passion I had felt, and I was pleased that I had felt angry for her.

Marek added some detail. "The scuff on Helena's phone was either a deflected bullet or caused by her fall. Either way, it damaged the RF side. It overheated while she was using it." I remembered the torch had still worked, but the failed radio explained why she had taken the bus rather than call for help.

Celestine covered her mouth in horror at the revelation that a shot had got quite so close to Helena, and burst into tears. Helena spent several minutes holding her, while the rest waited patiently. Again, there was no embarrassment, just a quiet pause.

"So—" Helena passed Celestine to Robert and looked round the table.

"So why didn't we just slip in and grab your bag from the skip?" I asked. "Why all the inspector stuff?"

"Because I needed to find out more. And you saw something was going on—how long Wuthers took to come down—and how cool he was about you searching the waste. That is, how cool he was until I suggested you look for chemical markers."

"So the whole 'biohazard' thing was just about judging his response to certain types of question?" I recalled how I had waved the pen around aimlessly.

Helena smiled. "I couldn't tell you in advance, James, I needed him to see your natural reactions." She turned back to Celestine and hugged her again, sandwiching the girl with Robert. "And I'm so sorry about picking up your test." Now everyone was looking elsewhere, so I chose not to stare either. That reminded me.

"But wait a minute, how did you do the phones? Wuthers called the number on the back of the magazine, and got through to Celestine. Surely you can't mess with the phone system like that?"

"No," Helena grinned, "we can't. But we *can* print a fake magazine. You saw me swap them in reception." I nodded as I replayed the whole briefcase and magazine business in my head, this time with a slightly different outcome.

"But, how did you know the receptionist would take it off you?"

"I didn't, that was a bonus. I just needed to draw her attention to it. Then I would have left it on her desk while I checked my make-up. She then gets the number from the 'advert' on the back cover, dials, Celestine answers, and voilà, we have our own Inspectorate."

I was impressed and I said so. She grinned more broadly, clearly pleased with the ruse. I suddenly recalled the print machine I had seen in the garage, and then the visit to the printers in town.

"So why did we visit those printers yesterday when you can print things here?"

"Oh, we didn't have the time to do it here, and we can't do the covers as well as they can. Besides, we needed ID cards too, and the printers doing it there saved a trip back here." I remembered my card, with its mugshot of an edited combination of the suit and haircut photos she had taken on her phone.

Helena breathed in deeply, ready to continue.

"So, here's the thing." Everyone drew closer. "I went with Wuthers and we inspected all floors of the building including the basement. The fifth floor was closed for building work, but I saw nothing unusual. Whereas in reception he was edgy, by the time we got to walk around he was relaxed, joking, not a care in the world." She frowned.

"Street wants answers. Today. I said we couldn't do that, but he's upped the fee for quick results, and he says the end of the week will be too late. No win, no fee. We have to get back in there." She paused again, pouting her lips. "Or maybe we don't need to get in physically. Access to their computer network might do it."

She turned. "Marek, how are we getting on with infiltrating their firewall?"

"Nothing yet. Maybe James can help me with that." She nodded approval. It felt good to have a job—I hoped I would not disappoint.

"Okay, and in that case, Robert you can look at those floppies? I thought they were out of place and they're the only thing I could grab before I got disturbed. James didn't find anything suspicious but couldn't open the actual files. Could you please give it a try?" He nodded. She turned to me and added "Robert's the only one with a working laptop old enough to have a floppy drive." Everyone laughed, even Robert.

"It's not actually my main computer, Helena." His tone suggested he had had to make that defence before.

"Whatever," she teased him. And then to us, "Okay, I will go and visit Mr Street at Zolotran. Maybe he has some ideas, and perhaps I can persuade him to be a bit more patient. You all know how it is—a client gets cold feet and then they don't pay."

Several gloomy faces told me this wouldn't be the first time this had happened. I sensed the urgency, but there was some housekeeping too.

"Um, is it okay if I use a car to nip home later and get some stuff?" Helena nodded.

"Take the Golf. At least I know you can drive that." I tried to look insulted. "But help Marek first, please."

Helena checked the others all had stuff they could do without her and then she was gone. I noticed everyone watched her leave. It was quite disconcerting.

13 – Problems before Lunch

Marek and I wandered out to his workshop and we sat down in his office, the giant printer brooding along the length of most of one wall. Although there was a double-width outside door, the printer must have been brought in in pieces and then re-assembled inside. Marek had promised to show me some of what it could do, later.

I sat beside him as he outlined me what he had found out about Pharmaply's network. He knew a lot, but they had spent considerable effort protecting themselves and the usual tools failed to get a foothold through their firewall.

We tried a few ideas together to probe their network, but without success. Then Marek set me up at my own desk and showed me how the phones worked. He took one look at my mobile and pulled a new one out of a drawer in his desk.

"Android, with 'improvements'." He used the same air quotes around improvements as Helena had. "Why not hang on to this while you're here?"

He opened the back. "Do you want to use your own SIM?" I shook my head, my credit was low and I didn't have any data allowance. He removed a card from the drawer, popped it in and powered up the device. Then he showed me how the phone worked both as a mobile and a local intercom when in Wi-Fi range. "I'll have to set you up." He returned to his desk to do so. "It will take a few minutes to propagate."

He plugged my new phone into his computer, and started a setup program to configure it. Then he took out his own phone, an identical model, and called Cleo on the intercom to show me how it worked.

"Hi Cutie," she answered.

He coughed. "I'm here with James, showing him how the phones work." There was giggling in the background.

"Hi, James." It took me a moment to realise the twins had answered in unison.

"Uh, hi," was all I managed, which resulted in more giggling. Marek cut them off mid-flow. He was smiling indulgently.

"Here, check this out," he said, moving on quickly. "If things go wrong, we need to know where people are, so Helena had this app made with a map."

It was a standard map, with a cluster of coloured dots at the centre. Marek pointed to the separate red dot on the main road. It was moving. "That's Helena, she's speeding." He sent her a text from his phone, reading as he typed "Nice app for gathering speeding evidence" and pressed send.

He touched the bottom left of the screen and the view changed, the cluster of dots spreading out. "Red is Helena," he pointed off screen. "This white one is Celestine, in her office." The walls of the house and outbuilding were displayed. "Purple is me, here with you." I had no dot. "Blue, is Robert, in the dining room. He tends to use the dining room when he's not at his office." Marek scrolled the map a little. "This dark green one is Alex in the garden, and the pink and light green are Cleo and Cat in the kitchen."

I interrupted him. "Cat and Cleo, are the colours, like, a thing."

"To tell them apart," he smiled. "Yes. We agreed it would help us mere mortals differentiate them, when they dress alike. As you saw last night, they often do different, but they also like to dress the same; it's like a twin thing—showing off that they *are* twins. And," he looked at me in warning, "they like to mix it up sometimes, dress the same, wear a pink or green headband or shoes or something to differentiate them, but then swap colours to confuse everybody. They love the little joke."

I pondered this and thought of him and Cleo. "So, is there any way to tell which is which, apart from fingerprints, retinal scans, and," my twin knowledge exhausted itself.

He smiled again. "Well there's knowledge—they probably

don't know exactly the same things, although sometimes I wonder."

"Any more?" I pressed.

"Well, indeed." He was evasive, but I could see he didn't want to discuss this further. A new flashing red dot appeared on the screen, which allowed him to change the subject. "So, what colour would you like to be?" Green was already oversubscribed, so I chose cyan.

Marek made the adjustment on his machine and a few seconds later the dot stopped flashing and turned light blue. I walked up and down the long office testing the accuracy of placement. It wasn't great, but it was good enough. "It's only GPS supplemented a little by Wi-Fi," he cautioned, "so the accuracy is only as good as the signal."

He paused uncertainly. "There is more to it, but," he waved his hands non-committally, "some other time." And with that he returned to his desk.

We worked separately for a couple of hours, him on the network, me on researching Pharmaply and Zolotran. I looked at my phone from time to time to see if the red dot was home yet.

***

Several tea breaks later, Marek came over again, this time to show me the internal layout of the house network. It was impressive, especially the knowledge base, an entire intranet of arcane documents and articles collected over the years. The log showed that much of the indexing and cross-referencing had been done by Celestine. A good indexer is hard to find, a librarian had once told me.

Just before lunch, Cleo called Marek out to help unblock a sink and with my research at a standstill, he suggested I explore a bit. Despite the occasional obvious hesitations, trust seemed to be a big thing here. I hoped I would not abuse it.

My first port of call was the old computer store again. The long narrow room had deep shelves and just enough space down the middle to carry things in and out.

Inside the door, to the left, was a small area with a workbench, covered with bits of kit. The shelves were like that too, a real graveyard of dead and maybe not-so-dead machines.

It was an eclectic mix.

I looked around at the mess, and thought I could make myself useful in the meantime by tidying up a bit. Things like the Toshiba could be useful if they could be located easily.

I found labels and markers in the office, and marked the first shelf on the left as 'working', and on the right 'non-working'.

I had just placed an old HP LaserJet on the bench when my phone beeped.

"Hello James." It was one of the twins' voices, but the phone said 'Marek'.

"Cleo?" I tried. There was a giggle.

"No."

"Hi Cat." A louder giggle.

"No."

I sighed. "Marek?" This produced a guffaw and another round of giggles. They were all there together and in unison they said:

"Lunch is ready."

I washed my hands and went into the house.

***

We were all there for lunch except Helena. Alex sat in her place, with Cat (possibly) to my left, and Cleo on my right, leaving a gap between her and Marek. I had glimpsed a green shoe on her, but remembered Marek's warning about the twins liking to fool people with the colours.

I suspected that we could have fed several more people on just the pasta alone, given the large glass bowl that held a mountain of rigatoni covered with a tomato sauce.

"Too spicy?" Cleo asked.

I shook my head. "No, it's delicious." And it was.

Afterwards, I helped clear the table, said my farewells and asked Marek to help me move the Golf out of the garage for my trip back home. As I made my way up the drive, much more slowly than yesterday, I glanced back at the house, nestling in the sun. It was a homely sight, so why did it make me feel slightly uneasy?

14 – An Old Life Revisited

Driving along the valley road in the Golf was effortless, easing my tension. I noticed I couldn't see over the hedges as I could from the bus. Occasionally I caught a glimpse of the river glinting in the sun through a farm gate.

Usually as I passed the sign for my village I would sigh, but today I felt light-hearted—a man with a purpose. Even the sight of my local bus stop failed to depress me.

I turned off the main road for the final quarter mile, and made an effort to drive carefully so as not to frighten the residents with the Golf's throaty roar. As usual, there wasn't anywhere to park. This was not a problem I had to solve too often, and it felt satisfying to have the challenge.

"I have a car," I said to myself, "I need somewhere to park."

I knew a spot just big enough right outside my landlady's driveway, but today someone had carelessly parked a white van there, and so I had to go round the corner to the newer part of the village and park alongside the row of modern terraces.

I put the top up, found my flat keys, and sauntered back, idly thinking about the past couple of days.

I should have noticed that the side door of the garage was open—it was the front door of my home. It's true that sometimes my landlady pops in to clean or to drop off laundry, but today was the day she played bowls, and normally she wouldn't leave the door ajar, nor slightly off its hinges.

Normally I'm more observant. As it was, I pushed the door further open before I realised the problem—two burly men looked up at me, their inherent meanness written all over their faces.

My coordination couldn't deal with the need to stop, turn, and run. Instead I sprawled over my own feet and nearly hit the mattress as I hit the floor, both sets of keys flying under the bed. The fall gave me a sudden rush of focus. I pushed the Golf's keys further under the bed, retrieved my flat keys, and lurched to my feet even as they approached me. There was no chance to run, but the adrenalin got me thinking fast. I wasn't good with my fists, but I knew how to play dumb.

"Hello," I said, as though their presence was entirely what I was expecting. I made a show of placing my own keys on the bedside table.

"Are you the new tenants?" They didn't looked confused, because that would have required a certain level of comprehension. The shorter of the two moved behind me to block any escape through the door. The larger was consulting his phone. After a few deliberate jabs, he peered at the screen and reached his conclusion.

"That's him," he nodded, convincing himself.

"Can I help you?" I tried.

"We need to have a little chat." I decided to call him Mr Large.

"Yes," echoed his slightly shorter friend. I decided he could be Mr Little. He came behind me and helped me to a seat on the bed.

In coming closer, he had left a gap to the door, and I considered making my break. But why they were here? I was annoyed and determined not to leave until I had some answers. I sat back a bit and let my jaw slacken to promote the idea of stupidity.

"Do you live here?" started Little. I considered playing with him a bit, but my annoyance was winning over curiosity so I simply nodded.

"So you is James Glass?" Another nod. This pleased the men. They looked like they had made a major breakthrough. Perhaps for them, this level of detective skill constituted a good day. I relaxed a little. While they could no doubt do me serious harm, they seemed more intent on intelligence gathering.

"And," continued Large, "last night, did you catch the Number 9 bus from New Road, in the city?"

They seemed remarkably well informed. I thought about what this might mean, while pretending to think about the bus.

After a suitable pause I led with "Ah, no, last night I was at my Mum's, I think. Yes, definitely, definitely at my Mum's." The gears turned slowly. Mr Large examined his phone.

"No, no, no, not last night, my mistake, the night before. Sunday night," he corrected. I made a show of considering the question again. If they had this much, they might have more, and some honesty now might make a little dishonesty more plausible later.

"Oh, yes, that's right. I did. It was raining." They looked at each other. Further success.

"And was you unwell, like sick or summat?"

I couldn't see where this was going, and two possible thoughts entered my mind. I decided to try option 'A'.

"No, not really." His face contorted. This clearly was not the right answer. Quickly I switched to option 'B'. "I guess I'd just had a bit much to drink." He looked much happier. Correct. "Yes, I definitely felt unwell." Dual nodding suggested they thought we were getting somewhere.

"So," Large continued, "take a look at this." He fumbled for a few moments with his phone and then turned it round. He wasn't good at holding it steady, but I had no trouble in recognising the video as the CCTV from a bus.

More precisely, the Number 9 bus of two nights ago. The screen was divided into four, one camera at each end of the vehicle, top and bottom. The picture was monochrome, with no sound, but Helena's dark hair contrasted well with her pale skin, and I easily recognised her arguing with the driver, and then me paying for her with my travel card.

The video replayed what I knew of the ride. The separate seats, me falling asleep at the back. I looked more closely as it continued to the bits of which I was unaware while I dozed in the back seat.

Soon after I fell asleep, Helena had walked to the back of the bus and nestled into me. It warmed my heart to see the simple affection she had shown.

Mr Large fast-forwarded a bit, which was annoying—I was enjoying the snuggle. Then Helena got up, moved to the front of the bus, talked to the driver. More hand gestures.

Finally she gave him something, and returned to my seat. More fast-forwarding. Finally, she shook me awake, and groggily I exited with her into the damp night. We had overshot her road, probably deliberately, and been dropped along a lane a couple of miles further in the valley.

"What's her name?" Mr Little demanded. It was still time to be honest.

"I'd never met her before."

"She told the bus driver she was your girlfriend." He drew himself up—he was very sure of this.

"What? Do you think someone living in a dump like this would have a girlfriend like *that*?" Both looked around at the meagre curtains; the bare light bulb; the grubby twin hotplate; the lack of door to the bathroom. The point was unarguable. Nevertheless, Mr Little tried.

"You paid her bus fare, we got your address from your bus card."

Well, that answered how they had found me.

Mr Large glared at Little for revealing too much information, and the shorter man went to investigate my keys. Satisfied with those, he motioned for me to stand with my arms out and he patted me down. He even missed the phone in my jacket pocket. I thought of the Golf keys, but I was careful not to look at the bed. I felt even more confident seeing their ineptitude. I tried to appeal to reason again.

"She didn't have change, I wasn't prepared to wait there all night while she argued. Besides, she was drunker than I was." A small lie to see how they took it. No reaction. I was satisfied that these two clowns knew very little about her and were just on a fishing expedition.

The taller one tried again. "We've asked the driver, she said she was your girlfriend and she bribed him fifty quid to turn off the main road to drop you both, because you were ill."

"Well, as you can see, I had passed out. But, I didn't ask her to bribe the driver, I was asleep before she did that. All I remember is she woke me up and hustled me off the bus and it wasn't even my stop!" This was all true, and I managed to deliver it with simple passion.

"So where is she? Wot happened after you got off the bus?" So, they knew nothing—I considered the possibilities.

Helena had been careful in making sure we were not dropped close to the house, hence the long walk back. Still, the best option was to place her away from the scene, distract them from searching that area. It was time to deliver the lie. I looked straight at them, the shorter one, then the taller one.

"She said she had a car. She offered me a lift to Weston. I remember telling her not to drive because she was drunk." I looked at them. Both were leaning forward and engaged in the story. I felt a little bolder.

"She suggested that I drive. There was a green car on the side of the road, a Vauxhall, I think. She got in the passenger side, but I fell over and ended up in the ditch, and by the time I got up, she was already driving away. She drove towards the main road."

They weren't completely satisfied, so I finished with a bit of indignation. "I walked to the road and hitched to my Mum's. Next morning I discovered the girl had stolen my wallet." This seemed to do the trick. Their nodding suggested this was what they expected of her. I decided to see how much more they knew. "Who is she?"

"She stole something."

"And my wallet too! What else did she steal?" But they

didn't know—they were just minions.

The sound of wheels-on-gravel announced the return of my landlady. The braking and ensuing door slam suggested she had had either a few bad ends at bowls, or was a bit miffed at having to dodge the van parked outside. Little and Large looked at each other.

Her feet made no noise on the flagstone path, but all three of us were counting down the seconds until she would inevitably fill the doorway.

"James? What's going on? Who are these men?" I saw my escape.

"Oh hi, Mrs Pettifer. They were just helping me move my desk. Sorry, seems we knocked the door a bit. They were just leaving actually." Her study of them suggested it would be a good thing.

Mr Large took the offering. "Yes, yes, we was just leaving," and with a jerk of his hand he and his slightly smaller self walked out.

I followed them out to continue the illusion of a sociable meeting, and thus managed to avoid difficult questions about the door. The two men pulled into the drive in order to turn around, and that's when I saw they had two furry pink dice hanging from the mirror. The colour didn't really match their attitude, but it gave me an idea.

15 – Tracking without Blood

Thankfully Mrs Pettifer had gone inside, and I sank down onto my bed to consider what had just happened.

The two bully boys had upset me. Who were they? Whose orders were they following? The high I had felt was waning. Having found me and heard my story, how long before they discovered the ruse and came back for more accurate information?

Hurriedly, I packed what I might need. It wasn't much. Everything fitted easily into one small bin bag, including my laptop. I unplugged my phone charger, and added it to the bag. I retrieved the Golf keys from under the bed.

It seemed a bit pointless to lock the door now, so I just shut it behind me as best as I could.

My spirits rose as I rounded the corner and saw the Volkswagen waiting for me, a burgundy promise of excitement and adventure.

I drove back to the house with a lot more care than I had taken on the way out. While the two goons had been harmless enough, I was sure they could be dangerous if the situation called for it, and given their limited executive function, they probably used violence rather than take the time to think things through.

I was sure they were after Helena, and I hoped I had done enough to get them off her scent. Nevertheless, I needed to warn her. Remembering the phone Marek had given me, I drove impatiently for a couple of miles before I could pull over into a lay-by.

I wondered about calling her direct, but I thought she might try to minimise the danger. Instead, I decided to call Marek. He listened carefully, but he wasn't as surprised or worried as I was. He took my concerns seriously, though, and said he would send her a message at once.

That off my shoulders, I was able to relax, and this got me

thinking about the video from the bus. It had showed Helena to be a very resourceful girl. I wondered how much of her cradling me in her arms was an act to fool the bus driver. Then I decided I didn't care. Any girl who wanted to hold me like that, just to fool a bus driver, was welcome to. Mr Logical woke up long enough to point out that she hadn't really needed to stroke my hair quite so much, so she was either putting on a very good show or being very forward indeed.

'Or you had done something to impress her,' Mr Grumpy added. I was surprised; I don't think he'd ever made a positive statement before.

I looked carefully in the mirrors before turning off the main road, but there wasn't a car in sight. As I came over the rise and saw the house lying in the afternoon sun, my heart sped up. I couldn't wait to tell Marek my idea.

He came out of the garage and waved as I pulled up. He suggested I park the Golf myself in the garage, but I told him we might need it.

I explained my theory and asked Marek if we had time to play with the Bugatti. He smiled at my enthusiasm, and led me over to the car.

"What about Pharmaply?" I was conscious of the deadline.

He smiled ruefully. "I'm stuck. A break might help. Let's see what you've got."

I pointed at the blue dice; they were an anachronism. Just as the fluffy pink dice had been out of kilter with the two thugs, so the blue ones had no place in a car like this.

The dice were attached to the car by thin black plastic wire. I had already figured out they had to be powered, because of the Eddie Murphy voice, but as Marek helped me carefully prise open the fairing that the wires disappeared into, it became clear there were more wires than were needed for power alone.

Two small holes for the wires had been drilled into the mirror's pillar, and with some more dismantling, we found the connections to the car's auxiliary power supply and internal network.

Marek was looking pleased. He jumped out to get the radio that he used as a lo-tech GSM detector, and turned it on while I carefully disconnected the wires. We both wondered if it would trigger while being dismantled, but silence ensued. Some of the wires connected the two dice together.

Once separated from the car wiring, I took the fluffy pair over to a bench and carefully slit open the first cube. From within the stuffing appeared a black plastic box, about the size of two matchboxes. The second dice revealed a similar enclosure, which turned out to be a battery. Eagerly I was about to examine the first box, when I remembered that this was Marek's domain. I passed it over to him, but he shook his head, refusing. "It's your idea, you do it." He sounded really chuffed to have been asked.

There were three little switches on the box, marked Power, CANbus and Voice.

Opening the box revealed a typical mobile telephone data module, a GPS receiver, and a microprocessor all on a single circuit board. One of the wires acted as an antenna for the GSM. The GPS antenna was below the circuit board. Reassembling the boxes, I tried the switches. With either the power switch or the voice switch off, Eddie was silent. With power and the voice button on, Eddie would speak if I tapped the box. He had a stock of about ten phrases.

I explained my theory. "The voice is just a distraction, just a bit of whimsy to hide the fact that the dice aren't completely soft." Marek nodded. "My guess is that the battery means it can run without the ignition on." Another nod.

"The GPS determines speed relative to the earth's surface, and the CANbus picks up engine data from the car network. Probably revs per minute and even what gear you're in to determine the car is actually moving on a road." Marek was grinning broadly. I could see he was itching to play, but his good manners prevailed.

"How will you test it?" is all he asked.

"I think the CANbus switch means that it will work without the engine data. We could try switching that off, and just taking the dice for a drive. If the cops pitch up, we're just driving a Golf."

***

Two hours later, we were back. Marek had driven the Golf a good distance away before I switched on the dice. Twenty-five minutes after that, we were rewarded with a squawk from the CB radio. Marek bounced in his seat, as I hastily switched off the tell-tale electronics. We hit the main road and he drove at a leisurely pace. If we had alerted anyone, we never saw them, and on a high, we pulled up once more to the house.

"Good job." Marek was really pleased. "It's taken months, but I think we're in a position to try the Bugatti outside again."

He left and I parked the Golf. It was tight, but the parking sensors helped. I picked up my bin bag of belongings and went inside to see what was cooking. The twins shooed me out of the kitchen and suggested I read the paper or a book in Helena's study. I wasn't sure about entering her sanctum but they assured me I had permission.

So, I took the bin bag to my room, and emptied it out onto the bed. It took just a minute to sort through the stuff. I put the clothes away, the laptop on the desk to charge, and I threw the phone charger into the drawer where my old phone lay. Somehow it looked even older and more beat-up than it had yesterday. It seemed to reflect my old life and as I walked back downstairs to Helena's study, I wondered if I could ever be happy with that life again.

Shortly afterwards I was again surveying the rich walls and paintings. The fire was glowing quietly. I stirred the clinker, and threw on a small shovelful of coal. Then I settled down to look through the books.

‘The Industrial Espionage Handbook’, one title proclaimed. This time it was a real book. I sat down in the armchair to learn something about an industry that I had managed, so far, to remain ignorant of.

16 – A Question of Street Cred

I was well into chapter three of the book when the door opened and Helena stood there, her hair reflecting the glow from the fire. She looked directly at me, a look that caused me to squirm and exult simultaneously. It felt as though her smile was lifting me physically out of the armchair, and I rose helplessly as she walked over and gave me a playful kiss on the cheek.

"Hello, clever," she led with. I think I blushed, and she gave me a hug. "Marek says if you can solve the Bugatti in 24 hours, then who knows what you might do in a week." I didn't need the praise, although it was good to hear it. She gave me another kiss, more directly.

This time, I was almost prepared as immediately afterwards she settled back into business mode. "Come on, council of war."

I followed the girl of my dreams—'in your dreams more like it,' Mr Grumpy contributed—to the hall. There she veered left and we entered a room as large as the living room, but minimally furnished. There were eight seats, a screen at one end, a bank of six large monitors on the adjacent wall, and two whiteboards opposite that. A free-standing lectern stood off to one side, so as not to obscure the screen.

Robert, Alex, Celestine, and Marek were already there. We appeared to be waiting for Cleo and Cat, so I took the opportunity to examine the monitors.

Helena coughed. I turned to see her glaring at me. The twins had arrived and I was now holding up the meeting. "Have you had enough ogling?" she asked sweetly. I sat down quickly and stared back hard at Helena, which I only managed because she wasn't looking directly at me.

"Okay," she started, moving to the lectern, "the pressure is on." Helena pressed a button and an image of the Pharmaply offices we had visited appeared on one of the monitors.

"What are Pharmaply doing to replace their ageing drug patent portfolio?"

She paused and the second monitor lit up. "That is the question that Xander Street, Zolotran's Chief Research Officer, is asking us." The man was no older than mid-thirties, but he had a hard, wily look to him. He knew how to dress, though. His suit probably cost more than a week's pay here.

"Marek has been unable to break through Pharmaply's firewall, even with wonder boy's help." She indicated me. Her tone was a little hard, and I wasn't sure if she was being sarcastic. I looked across to where Robert was seated and saw him beaming, so I figured it might be okay.

"Really good job on the Bugatti," Helena added gently.

Everyone clapped at that, and I was embarrassed. Cat leaned over to give me a kiss on the side of my neck, and a squeeze.

"We really need to get past that firewall, and if we can't do that, we need to physically gain access to the server room to compromise the firewall from within. We *need* to analyse their data." Helena bit her lip and turned to Marek. "How long to bypass a firewall with physical access from within?"

He shrugged. "Who knows. Probably an hour if they've used a simple password. Maybe less if they've left it under the keyboard.

"Maybe several days if they know something about security." He looked at me. We both knew the firewall setup had looked very professional so far. It was unlikely to be a quick break-in.

Helena put up another picture, this time of the building from the air. "This is a satellite image. This single-storey extension houses the accounts department.

"On its roof," she pointed to three cooling fans, "are heat exchangers, probably for the air-con in the server room which we therefore think is on the first floor here." A side view of the building appeared; the wall beyond the extension was devoid of windows. "During my 'inspection' I looked down that corridor and saw that security was tight. I doubt we can just walk in there, even if we gained access to the building. Last time I tried that, people started shooting. I doubt we could get in there undetected for an hour, let alone days."

She paused, pressed the button on her remote a few times, and images appeared of the building from different angles, together with more satellite imagery of the surrounding area. She turned to the room and asked, "Any ideas?"

Everyone studied the photos in professional silence.

I was wondering about a fake fire, when Marek said, "We could do a quick break-in, steal a server, and analyse it back here, but they would know there was a problem. And we might not pick a useful one."

Helena thought about this, but I was staring at the satellite imagery of the wider area. "What's on the other side of the river?" I asked.

"It's a stream, not a river, and they're just industrial units." Helena replied in a tone that suggested I was going off at a tangent, but Marek had seen the gleam in my eye and he settled back in his seat, preparing to enjoy the ride.

I stood up and pointed to the monitors. Helena gave me a laser pointer and I indicated the flat roof of the extension. "This roof is only twelve feet up or so, and there is no fence on the river side.

"The *stream*," I corrected, seeing Helena's glare, "doesn't look very wide. The same extension ladder might do for both." I explained the basics of my idea, and everyone chipped in with refinements. Finally Helena asked the twins to ensure that supper could be a movable feast, and we set off to prepare.

***

Ninety minutes later, Robert, Alex and I moved cars around the garage until we had a blue minibus and two vans out. One of the vans was a grey Kombi—half bus, half van, with dark tinted windows on the sides, ideal for surveillance. The other was completely white, an ordinary man-and-van van.

Robert showed me where the ladders were, and helped me lift two of them onto the Kombi roof rack.

Alex called me and asked me to help her outside Marek's office. I shifted some steps for her and held them as she rooted around upstairs and came down with several pairs of paper overalls in different colours. She decided on dark navy, and passed me one. Then she handed me five other pairs.

Balaclavas followed. "New stock each time," she explained. "We burn the clothing after, reduces the evidence." Not cheap, I thought, but she said they didn't burn the rather nice radios she was handing me. She handed me a pair of socks and made me try on boots.

Cat, or Cleo—it was hard to tell as she was now barefoot—appeared and, seeing what we were doing, asked Alex to get down a few more pairs of the paper overalls for painting their ceiling. Alex rolled her eyes and shooed her off, but promised she would. She gave the girl two pairs of boots and socks.

As I left Alex, Celestine joined her and they were firing up the printer and the big iMac computer sitting next to it.

Marek was loading kit into the Kombi. He had already installed a sophisticated camera on a remote control mounting so it could see out of one of the side windows. It was hooked up to several rack-mounted units that held the mobile networking. He showed me a zone pressure microphone with its square plate, bigger than my hand, and its rugged transmitter. A small portable camera completed the surveillance ensemble. I nodded my approval.

I handed out the clothing. Alex hadn't needed to consult a list to get the sizes—I wondered how often they did this sort of thing. This minor distraction meant I was caught by surprise as everyone changed right there. Slightly more surprising was a marked lack of undergarments.

"James." Helena, now dressed, sounded very matter-of-fact. "Anything you wear now will be burned later, so if you don't want to lose it later, lose it now." I thought of my new boxers, and although I hadn't paid for them, I was not in a hurry to just throw them away. I chickened out by going round the van to change.

"Hurry up James," teased Helena, "we need to get there before the security shift change happens at seven!"

Celestine came out to see us off, holding a set of small plastic crates. We each put our old clothes in one then Helena did a quick check that we had loaded everything that we might need into the Kombi. Celestine gave her a peck on the cheek, looking at me warily as she did so.

Helena drove the Kombi and I rode shotgun. I had started to fold down one of the jump seats behind Helena because the twins were jammed in the front, but Helena told them there wasn't enough room, and made them swap with me.

As they got out I noticed their laces were undone, but whereas mine were brown, they were sporting green and pink between them.

I made the mistake of pointing this out to Helena, and there was a slight scuffle from the back. I turned to see the twins plant their boots firmly to the right of my ear, each now sporting one pink lace and one green one. They pulled their tongues out at me in perfect synchronisation.

Helena, looking in her rear-view mirror, smiling knowingly, as we set off down the drive.

17 – Things Heat Up

About thirty minutes later, we were parked behind the industrial units, across the stream from Pharmaply. Several large containers and half a dozen parked vehicles provided reasonable cover, although we were the only people around.

Marek's first job was to get a jack from the van and push it under the Kombi. He raised it slightly, without actually touching the bus, to look as though we were changing a tyre. When he unpacked a flat tyre and a wheel spanner from the boot, I knew he had done this before. He smiled. "If we have to leave in a hurry, we just drive off leaving a jack and an old tyre."

Then he helped me remove the first ladder from the roof and extended it. The stream was more a large ditch six metres across, with the actual water about a metre down. It didn't look like deep water, but the bed looked very muddy. We picked a spot where bushes on the other side provided some cover. After a quick look around to check we were unobserved, we placed one end of the ladder on our side and then dropped it over the ditch, creating an instant bridge.

We settled down to wait for the security guard changeover. Just before seven we saw an old Ford Escort drive up and Helena decided it was time. We put on our balaclavas and took our chance.

The ladder-bridge was not very stable. I had the bolt cutters and Cat was carrying a small canvas bag. Cat crossed the ladder as though it were a solid path. When she saw me struggling, she left her bag and came back for the bolt cutters, so I could cross on all fours. Marek then followed, carrying the smaller ladder over his shoulder. Another look around and we broke from the cover of the bushes and sprinted for the building. A few seconds later we were tucked behind the admin extension. Marek and Cat still had their breath; I was panting.

Marek put his ladder up against the wall of the single story block. Cat handed her bag to Marek, took the bolt cutters and climbed onto the flat roof.

Marek and I made our way to the front of the building, sprinting hard to get there before the guards finished changing.

We stopped just before the transparent reception part of the building. We were situated behind the side of the glass slab of the reception desk with a good view across it. The two guards were a few feet in front of it, exchanging pleasantries. Marek took the zone microphone out of the bag, and, peeling back the sticky tape, pressed it up against the glass where it wouldn't be seen from the inside. The whole of the plate glass window was now acting as a giant microphone.

"Helena," Marek whispered.

"I've got it, Marek," I heard in my ear. "I can hear them clearly." I positioned the mobile camera so it too could see through the glass wall. I aimed it at the talking guards, but Helena asked for a wider view to include the back of the reception desk. I made adjustments. I could see the Pharmaply CCTV monitors hidden behind the desk.

We rushed back to the foot of the ladder, climbed onto the roof, and dragged the ladder up behind us so we could hide if necessary. A minute later Helena's voice whispered in my ear. "All looks quiet from here." I rose a little and waved in her direction. "Yes, I can see you idiot, which means they probably can too." I crouched down again trying to look sheepish, but actually I felt completely alive.

We crossed the roof carefully. The first fan unit hummed gently, a waft of warm air blowing out of its heat exchanger. I showed Cat the big red and yellow rotary switch that turned off the fan's power, and the hole where you could put a padlock to stop people just switching them off. They hadn't bothered with locks—the bolt cutters were not needed.

We made sure that each of the other fans was similarly

unlocked, and then Marek and I climbed back down, leaving Cat on the roof. She pulled the ladder back up again. Helena confirmed the guard wasn't behind his desk yet. We took a breath, then sprinted for the stream. It had all taken less than ten minutes.

We lay low for a while, and Marek used the time to check the camera in the dark-windowed Kombi. He pointed it at the rear of the building where we could see most of a loading bay including the skip I had played in on my first visit. He showed me the video disk recorder and how the live feed, broadcast over mobile internet, could be controlled from his phone, allowing him to zoom, pan, and tilt to look at whatever might be of interest.

We rehearsed once more, and then Helena radioed Cat to turn the fans off. From where we were, we could hear the clunk of the industrial switches, and then the decreasing drone of the fans as they spun down.

A monitor had been set up in the bus, showing a clear picture of the reception desk from the camera we had planted. The microphone taped to the glass clearly amplified every sound the guard made as he settled into his chair. It only took a few seconds after the fans stopped for an alarm to sound in reception.

"Now let's see what they do," Helena muttered to herself. Marek plugged his phone into the receiver. He opened an app to listen to the audio.

"Good picture," I said, to no one in particular. It really was very clear.

"High def," Helena boasted. Marek looked at her as though he didn't consider HD to be newsworthy. Helena stuck out her tongue at him, without removing her eyes from the screen. We watched as the guard sauntered to the end of the reception desk and pressed something. The alarm noises stopped. He reached under the desk where we could see another phone, put it on speaker, then dialled.

Helena looked at me, and gave a theatrical chuckle. Marek's phone displayed the dialled digits as each beep was heard. A quick internet search gave us the air-con company's name even before they had answered the phone.

While the guard reported the fault, Helena called Alex and Celestine back at home. "It's Maple Air," she said, and read out the number. "We'll confirm when they get here."

As it was, it only took twenty minutes until a white van with an eye-catching paint job of multi-hued red and orange leaves drove up and parked in front of Pharmaply. A man got out, wearing white overalls.

Helena redialled Alex. "Tell Celestine the van is just like the image on the web. And the guy is wearing white overalls, looks like a reddish logo top left pocket area. No cap. Robert will send pictures now."

We watched as the security guard took the engineer through reception and out of sight. Helena counted twenty seconds then told Cat to switch the fans back on. Ten minutes later, the two men were back in reception. The guard showed the engineer the panel and the latter shrugged and walked back out to his van, and drove away.

We waited until the guard was back at his desk, then Helena dialled the Pharmaply number. We heard the phone ring, and saw the guard pick it up.

"Pharmaply, good evening."

"Good evening." Helena sounded the sort of affected posh you might get on night shift. "This is Julie from Maple Air. Our engineer has just reported that he's looked at your air-con and didn't find a fault. I'm just calling to see if you are satisfied with our response." The guard professed himself content.

"I understand the fault was in the, er, sieve room."

"The *server* room," he corrected her, indulgently.

"Oh, sorry," and she gave a little 'I'm just a girl' laugh. "And did the engineer check the server room?" This was confirmed. Helena beamed. "Well, he told me he's left the monitor on, so if you have any more problems, don't hesitate to call," she finished sweetly and hung up. The Cheshire Cat would have felt envious of her grin.

***

It was almost completely dark by the time Alex and Celestine arrived in the minibus, and we had to stir ourselves again.

Helena set us to work. Robert wiped down the left side of Marek's van with a cloth while Celestine had me hold the sheets of plastic film that she had just printed. Cat and Cleo knew how to peel them and, starting at the bottom, Celestine and Marek worked their way along the van, smoothing the film down, transforming the winter whiteness into the autumnal russets and golds of Maple Air. Celestine smiled at me for the first time since I had met her and said, "Photoshop and the Internet—a match made in heaven." I smiled back—the van looked great.

I moved round to the other side, expecting to repeat the performance, and then saw everyone looking at me, waiting for the penny to drop. Of course, the guard would only see one side. I deserved the laugh.

Alex had brought new overalls to match the air-con engineer. The logo was printed on a canvas-looking paper, and then embroidered round the edge to make it more 3-D. They looked the real deal. Alex passed one of these new creations to me, and one to Marek.

This time, I didn't bother with going round the side of the van to change, and the studied silence was quite intimidating. Alex handled us a pair of gloves each to complete the outfit.

We checked our toolboxes and Helena signalled Cat. "Turn them off."

Again we heard the familiar wind-down as the fan power was cut. We all watched the monitor: the guard got up, and moved towards the alarm panel. Helena dialled. He had just silenced the alarm as the phone in reception rang.

Helena performed that strange neck stretch people do before swinging into action, and then started speaking.

"Hello, it's Julie again from Maple Air. Our monitor has just reported another fault. Do you have that?" The guard said he did. "Well, I'll send a crew right away," she promised. "I've got Joe and Sam, they aren't far away." I spluttered and nearly laughed out loud at the truth of that, but Helena's look was an effective deterrent.

"They might need some help checking the panel; would you be able to help them with that?" The guard assured her he could. She thanked him and concluded the call. We waited five minutes, then Marek and I jumped into the van and worked our way round the industrial estate and back to the Pharmaply front entrance.

We pulled up a little further back than our predecessor had, to ensure there was no view of the back of the van from reception. It was like watching a television replay as the security guard met us at the door, and showed us through.

Introductions were made. "Joe, Sam." "Pete."

As we walked across reception, I gave a grin in the direction of the camera outside. There was a low wolf-whistle in my ear—I nearly blushed.

Helena took advantage of the distracted guard and sent Cleo to retrieve the microphone from the glass and the mobile camera from outside reception. I heard her tell Cleo to wait for Cat behind the admin block.

The security guard took Marek and me up in the elevator to the first floor. I could see Marek studying the layout carefully as I engaged 'Pete' in chatter about the football. He let us through two sets of doors secured with a card reader, before we stopped in front of another door marked 'Authorised Personnel Only' in bold red letters. This time he needed a key and a card. The door opened, and Pharmaply's corporate server room lay before us, a miniature galaxy of glowing LEDs in the semi-darkness.

The guard switched the lights on, and the galactic effect diminished somewhat, but not by much. Bay upon bay of computer racks were lined up in neat rows. If they knew their stuff there was no doubt a mirror installation at some other site for redundancy, but we had no time to admire it.

This was a critical moment—neither Marek nor I knew much about air conditioning. Marek looked at me. I cleared my throat and was about to ask the scripted question of 'which panels did the other engineer check', when the guard demonstrated his helpfulness by showing us. It didn't help a lot. Three red lights marked 'fan failure' were on.

"Hmm," I said to Marek meaningfully, "fan failure."

He nodded, and asked the guard, "Is there a phone in here?" The guard shook his head. Marek pulled a pair of cheap walkie-talkies out of his bag, showed the guard how to use one, and asked if he would mind checking the panel downstairs.

As soon as he was gone, we looked around. We didn't have long. It wasn't possible to tell which of the bays held what, but all we needed was a space to link into the network.

Marek selected a glass-fronted bay near the outside wall that held a large network patch panel and switches. The patch panels brought wires from network points in the building and the switches joined them all together into one logical whole. Smaller bays on each floor would further distribute the network. Marek opened the bay, and also its neighbour.

I took a Wi-Fi transceiver out of my toolbox, and put it into the second cabinet. I plugged the power in, and fed the ethernet cable through to Marek who plugged it into a spare socket on the patch panel. Just above that, a little LED lit up on one of the switches to indicate we had just added our own Wi-Fi access point to the very heart of Pharmaply's data network.

Helena tested the connection from her end. It took a few seconds for the kit in the Kombi to connect, and once she announced that data was flowing, Marek closed the bays. We were wondering how long the guard could take to get downstairs when the radio crackled.

"I'm here."

Marek asked him how many lights were on.

"One green, three red."

"Okay, hang on a second there, Pete." We heard Helena tell Cat to power up one of the fans, and we heard the first unit start to wind up.

"What about now?" Marek asked.

"Two green, two red." The guard sounded pleased. Helena paused dramatically before asking Cat to switch on the second fan. After another pause, the guard reported he had all green lights.

"Hey Pete," said Marek, "come let us out, will ya? It's getting kind of cold up here."

While we waited for Pete, Marek pulled out a padded envelope from his tool bag and took out a small piece of charred copper cable. He showed this cable to Pete when he relieved him of the radio. "Probably caused by a mouse. Shouldn't have any more problems now."

As we were leaving the server room, Helena told us that Cat and Cleo were making their way back from the roof with the ladder.

We drove back round, and started packing up.

Marek and I retrieved our temporary bridge from across the stream while the others loaded up the spare kit into the white van. Celestine's creation had been stripped off in seconds, leaving no trace of Maple Air.

Marek and I entered the Kombi to check the network both to Pharmaply and to the wider internet. We also checked that the Kombi's camera feed was still accessible from his phone. The others were piling into the minibus.

My heart was racing.

18 – A Slightly Bigger Box

It was nearly ten by the time we had parked everything in the garage, and dumped all the clothes in the incinerator. We were all hungry, and everyone was buzzing.

Cleo served a fondue with what she called 'York bread'—day-old baguette which absorbed the cheese beautifully.

Glad to be back in my own clothes, I was one of the first there, but before long happy munching was accompanied by the pop of corks as Robert opened two bottles of white and started pouring.

As promised, Alex produced some paper overalls for the twins to do their painting. Cat informed everyone that tomorrow's breakfast would be 'do it yourself'. The twins' persistent attempts to get me to help them paint were halted when Helena appeared in the doorway.

"I'm sorry," she said, "I think I probably need to get out for a while." She waved a hand vaguely and the others looked understanding. I had been thinking more about the possibility of getting to sleep early. Or at least today. Or perhaps not exactly sleep. Helena interrupted my reverie by asking me if she could have a quick word in her study. She allowed me to walk past her, remaining a moment before following me.

It felt funny to hear her walking lightly behind me, and I felt closely watched as I opened the door to the panelled room, holding it open for her. The fire was bright and cheerful but I felt apprehensive with the unexpectedness of this formal meeting.

She sat me on the armchair and then sat on my lap, wrapping her arms around my neck. Not quite as formal as I had expected.

"You did a good job tonight—" she kissed me "— it was a great plan." I basked in her praise. I was only just starting to come down off the high generated by our escapade, and so I kissed her back. I hoped she'd take the hint, but when she didn't I tried again. She pulled back from me, suddenly serious.

"James, it's getting a bit late, and I think I know what you hope will happen." I nodded. She was being very careful.

She looked around as though there was an easier way to break the news. I rapidly reworked the evening, wondering if I had messed up at some point. Smiling, she returned my gaze and, taking a deep breath, launched into her explanation.

"You know I said couldn't be yours one hundred per cent?" I must have looked very alarmed because she nuzzled into me and giggled. "Don't be an idiot, I'm not trying to get rid of you." I decided I didn't mind being *her* idiot.

"I just also have other responsibilities. Other people I have to look after. Other people ... I love."

Two thoughts collided and for a moment I wondered if Mr Grumpy and his cohorts were back. The first thought was 'she loves other people', and I felt a dread that I might lose her to them. The second followed like a large wave crashing over the first, swamping it completely, and most comprehensively. This was the realisation that the word 'other' was only needed if I was one of those that she loved. I had no idea how to handle such an expression of affection, and I only managed a pitiful grunt.

To her credit, she didn't slap me for my crassness. She just stood up, ruffled my hair and told me she had to go out. Off to party with friends, I thought. I stood up to say goodbye. She kissed me again.

"It works both ways, James. You're free to explore other relationships too." I didn't dare tell her the likelihood of that happening was slim. She tried again. "Well, at least help Cat and Cleo with their ceiling." I nodded, looking sad, and she ruffled my hair again. Then with a wistful look, she left me.

I sat down, and had a little think.

***

By the time I arrived back in the drawing room, everyone had left, except Alex who was finishing a cup of tea. She smiled as I entered, and when she saw my woeful look, she patted the chair beside her and said, "Come and sit." So I did.

After a minute or so, she turned to me.

"What is it you want, James?" she asked quietly.

I looked at her. How to explain the meaninglessness of my life up until two days ago? Just two days! The reality was I was having a hard time catching up. I knew Mr Grumpy and Mr Logical for what they were—friends in a friendless world—and how quickly I had managed to abandon them once someone else even smiled at me.

How to explain that I had never really connected with girls, and then suddenly meeting the most amazing—no, most outrageous girl that I could never have dreamed of, who was funny and smart and serious and whose mood changed so rapidly—only to find out she was not really mine at all. I didn't know where to start. I sat there staring at my knees.

Alex lifted my chin and smiled again. It was a very engaging smile. I smiled back. "Where do you live?" she tried again.

I told her about the garage; a little bit of my childhood; about work.

"But no girls." She didn't ask, she just stated. I shook my head. "And what is it that you think people generally want?" She was probing, leading me somewhere.

"Somewhere nice to live, a good job, friends." I started, then faltered as I realised I was describing this place. "Maybe a wife—" and seeing her enquiring eyebrows I corrected myself quickly "—or lover."

She nodded, and looked down into her lap, gathering her thoughts. I expected the silence to be awkward, but it wasn't. Maybe it was the afterglow of the adrenaline, but somehow the stillness was like a blanket, wrapped around me, holding me, warming me. I waited, patiently.

She looked up, making sure I was ready. I took a deep breath, prepared myself for some bad news. But when she spoke, even though I didn't really like the words, they were like a lance for the pain I felt.

"House, job, friends, a lover," she repeated the list back to me, nodding to affirm my choice. "Imagine, James, that you had all those things.

"Even if you did, you don't *own* them. They are free to come and go. Even a house, if you own it, you own it for only a few years." I nodded, and wondered what her point was. I realised I didn't own Helena, but to be losing her before I really even found her seemed so hard.

"And of those things you've listed," Alex continued, "which do you think we have here?"

I shrugged, "Nice place to live, work seems reasonable, maybe a bit dangerous." She smiled, and I realised she didn't consider danger to be a good reason not to do something. I continued. "You seem to like each other. Maybe Marek and Cleo ..." I trailed off. I had been about to say Marek and Helena.

Alex was nodding. "Yes, James, that's what we have here. Work, home, friends, lovers." I looked at her. The word *lovers* was unexpected, but maybe explained a few things. She was watching me keenly.

"None of us are related by DNA—the twins aside—but we are like one big family. Not mum and dad and little sister, we're all more like ... cousins."

I thought about this a few seconds, and then recognised the euphemism. "You mean as in *kissing* cousins."

Her mouth twitched, and I realised her smile was starting to awaken the dancers in my back. "Cousins don't just kiss," she corrected me.

"So Marek and Cleo?" She nodded. I thought a little longer. "Come on," she encouraged me, "you're good at thinking outside of the box." She drew a rectangular outline with her fingers.

"Yes, but when people say 'think outside the box', in my experience, they just want a slightly larger box."

She nodded, "But that doesn't apply here. So, go wild. Think." She drew her hands apart, stretching the imaginary container.

"Robert and ..." I was about to say 'you', but I realised that might be rude or too obvious, "and Celestine?"

She shrugged. "Maybe not, but maybe Cat, sometimes." My eyes widened. This was proving to be an education in itself.

I dived in. "But then Helena and Marek." She nodded, and then spread her hands again, making the box even bigger. I was confused, but trying hard to be generous at the same time. "So Helena went out just now with Marek?"

She looked very patient, "Now, this is not lateral thought, James! Marek is upstairs, Cat and Cleo are painting. Robert's gone for a shower, I'm here. Who was missing in the drawing room?" It took me only milliseconds.

"Celestine? Helena and *Celestine*?" She was looking at me. Just watching my reaction. I wasn't sure how to react. Mr Logical did the kind thing and jumped to my rescue. 'If you're going to share,' he asked me, 'then why not with a girl?'

I mulled this for a moment, and then I smiled, and Alex did so too, glad that I had made it over the road bump.

"So how does it work? This non-exclusive thing?" I hoped it wasn't a rude question.

Alex gave a little laugh at my discomfort. "If you fancy someone, ask them. If they say no, move on gracefully, no moods, no sour grapes."

"And anybody can go out and meet anybody?"

She shook her head. "No, it's non-exclusivity within in the family, but no outside interactions. It's just not safe these days."

"But, I'm not a member of the family."

Her fingers traced another box shape. "You are on

probation, we all voted for you last night." She was amused that I had forgotten these facts.

"I thought it was a job interview." I was trying to keep up. "Anyway, what about me? Don't I get a choice?"

She laughed openly now. "Of course you do. If you said no, then this would just have been a job interview. And given your talents, I can see Helena would ask you to come back when you can, to help."

That sounded okay.

"But that is why I asked you what you wanted, James. Because if you want, and if this"—she searched for another word and then just said it—"probation; if this probation goes well, then you will get to choose between this and whatever else you have.

"If you *want* to, and if we want to, then you can choose to have this as your home, as your family. Friends definitely, and if you like and they like, then maybe a lover. Or two."

I suppose if I had been able to imagine my wildest dream, it would not have been this wild. Maybe I wasn't so good at thinking outside of the box after all.

"So I have a choice."

I spoke more to myself, in the realisation that while the choice existed, it was like offering a drowning man not just a rope, but an entire yacht. Except he'd have to share. And no sour grapes.

I suddenly remembered the commotion yesterday morning near the stables. "But Celestine was mad with Helena because she saw Helena with me."

Alex shook her head, "No, Celestine was mad with Helena, because Helena had left her waiting an entire night while she just 'popped into town for a quick trip to Pharmaply'. She should have been back in less than two hours. Not only did Helena forget she had kept Celestine waiting, she then brought home a random stray instead." I could see how that must have looked.

"Helena didn't break the exclusivity code." I wanted her to understand.

"We know, she told us. Bit rough on you," she smiled. "And don't forget Celestine did vote for you last night too."

"She didn't look happy."

"She wasn't then, but she hadn't had a chance to see you in action, and she didn't see what Helena saw on Sunday night."

"Which was?" I winced as I realised this was potentially fishing for a compliment.

"Bright, resourceful, gentle, paying attention to detail," she stopped and then added, "and lost." I exhaled, that single word summed me up completely. My heart melted again thinking of the girl who had noticed.

I nodded, my mind made up. "I understand how it works. But, it doesn't make it easier, right now."

She stood, patient. "Why don't I take you to find the twins? I'm sure they could use some help and it will take your mind off things."

I nodded, grateful, and she smiled. That was definitely working on me. As she led the way upstairs I found myself focussing on the carpet more than was strictly necessary.

19 – Cats on the Ceiling

Alex stopped outside a room that seemed to be on the opposite side of the house to mine, and knocked. There was a squeal within, followed by a laugh, and a few seconds later the door opened a crack. A white-covered elf peeked out. Even her hair had a paper covering like a shower cap. "Hello," the elf greeted us.

"James has come to help you," Alex informed her. "Helena said I was to tell you to make sure you look after him."

"We will," the elf replied, "but first he has to change or he'll mess up his clothes." The Cat/Cleo elf disappeared for a moment and then a white paper overall was thrust into my hand together with a hat. I looked around. They looked at me. I sighed. I supposed I would have to get used to this. I changed right there.

Alex offered to dump my clothes in my room on the way down. I thanked her, and then realising how grateful I was to her, bent over and gave her a kiss. I aimed for her lips, but approached with caution. She waited, guiding me in with her eyes, shutting them as we made contact. It was a good kiss. I wondered if I was letting an opportunity pass, but she decided for us by gently pulling away. I watched her leave and then turned back towards the elf who was watching me with a raised and much amused eyebrow. "Ready?" she asked.

I blushed. I wondered if I was going to get over the blushing.

The room I entered was as large as mine, maybe a little longer. Currently it sported freshly painted walls in a pale Devon-cream, but no carpet, and the floorboards were covered with a combination of paint-splattered dust covers and polythene sheet.

"We lost a bit of roof in those storms during March," the elf explained. "It brought down the ceiling and ruined the carpet. We've only just had the ceiling fixed."

I was surprised to see a large bed in the centre of one wall, also plastic covered. Beside the bed, holding a paint roller on a long handle, was Cat. I knew it was Cat because she was facing me and she had the word 'Cat' on the front of her overall, written sideways, from top to bottom. The large letters were interestingly translucent.

"It's baking spray." Cleo laughed. "When we were cooking earlier, Cat noticed it makes paper almost see-through." I could certainly see through, but the lettering had been applied so artistically, that it wasn't until you got to the tail of the 't' that there was any hint of indiscretion. At least I can tell them apart, I thought to myself as Cleo handed me the roller and helped me put my hair cover on.

As we turned to paint, I noticed one of them also appeared to have sat in baking spray. I could guess which one.

We worked methodically. Cleo could manage without tape, so she used a ladder and we let her cut in the edges with a brush, while we followed behind and filled in the larger expanses with rollers.

The work wasn't taxing—they could have done it without me—but it allowed me to think, and there was lots to think about.

I noticed the twins exchange glances from time to time, but we mostly worked in silence, except where one of us would point out a missed spot.

***

Fifty minutes later, I removed the last accidental splash from the wall and we were done. The twins lay down on the floor to admire our work for a minute, and they were delighted.

Cleo wrapped the rollers in plastic film. I offered to help clean them but she explained they would keep better like this until the next coat. However, the brushes needed cleaning so she took them down to the scullery in a black bin bag to sort out. Cat waited until she had gone, and then sat on the edge of the bed.

"Tell me what Alex said," she offered, by way of an ice-breaker.

I sat down next to her and thought for a moment. She took my hand. I was floundering in a sea of unknown emotions and I didn't know how to start. Instinctively I minimised what I was feeling. I shrugged and said, "Nothing."

Cat looked at me, but I was staring at the floor. Lucky for me, she didn't let go.

"Why not start at the beginning?"

Mr Logical assisted and I let him start by listing the facts as I had encountered them. It helped me to see the whole picture again. I summarised: "So, you're not just work colleagues."

"No," she laughed ruefully and I appreciated her self-deprecation, "we think of ourselves as family. We work well together, and sometimes we play together." She paused and then added with a little shrug, "Well, more than sometimes." She looked at me and I smiled as I looked at her. Her honesty was beguiling.

"And what are you thinking?" she continued. Her voice had dropped a little, and she was moving carefully. Not warily, not afraid *of* me. More afraid *for* me, I thought.

I sat looking at the floor for a full minute. She gave me the space then stood up.

"Come, let's go and clean up in the shower, and we can talk."

I wasn't sure.

"Besides, I need someone to help me wash my hair."

It was a good line. Irrefutable, and appealing directly to Mr White Knight, but I found myself wondering what Helena would think.

"And Helena said you had to look after us, remember?" I harrumphed. This was a blatant re-write of recent history, and I was about to protest but laughed instead, realising I was being churlish. I followed her across the room.

I wasn't surprised that the twins had their own en suite, nor that Cat dropped her overall and hat in the bedroom before entering. I was slightly surprised that while still more than generously sized, the bathroom wasn't as palatial as mine. It was definitely narrower, and had only a single toilet and no bidet. This puzzle resolved itself even as I pondered it, for Cat continued right through, and what I thought was the bathroom turned out to be a mere antechamber for the shower room, larger than the bedroom itself.

My room's shower looked like an afterthought compared to this. Two-tiered wooden benches sat in opposite corners, one closed off by a curved screen to make a steam room, the condensation trickling down inside of the glass walls. The benches on the other side looked like they were for just sitting. Or watching.

Instead of shower heads, there was a continuous array of pipes. Cat touched the control panel, and pointed to others around the room. "You can control anything from anywhere," she said, as a curtain of water started to tumble from the pipe matrix, a miniature waterfall.

She showed me some of the choices available. "This is a later version than Helena's and yours," she said with pride. "We use it as the family bathroom." Enough for a football team, I thought, as I explored the options.

I liked the look of the shoulder massage. Cat led me to one side where chrome steel bars were curved to support the front of the body. She showed me how to stand, leaning forward slightly, so my back was positioned under a thick stream of slightly pulsing water. Other jets added interest, and I found myself able to relax against the warm bars, with my arms flopped over the top.

"You must use lakes-full of water," I commented and she smiled. The jets had adjusted to accommodate her shorter body as she 'lay' next to me, not quite touching.

"It's recycled unless you choose 'clean', silly." I nodded; of course it was.

The jet between my shoulder blades was doing some serious work. I closed my eyes, enjoying the sensation. I heard her move on to the bars on my other side, and I opened my eyes to see why. She smiled and I smiled too. A laugh made me look back. She hadn't moved; another elf had simply appeared. Or they had swapped. Looking left and right at the amazing stereo effect I really could see no difference at all. They returned my appraisal with open faces.

They were waiting. Giving me time. I realised I had to make the first move. I let the water pummel my shoulder blades, took a deep breath, and started the conversation.

"So, you're family?" They giggled. Okay, it wasn't much of an opening line. I tried again. "Where did you meet Helena?"

"At university." I looked surprised; there was a distinct age gap.

"You were at university together? But you're, like, ..." I realised this was a bear trap of massive proportions. Mr Logical suggested that a wise man would have kept his mouth shut. One of the girls rescued me.

"We're twenty-four. And we were studying at St Andrews, Cleo did maths"—Okay, that told me Cat is still on my left —"and I did biology. Helena was working as a receptionist there."

"Did you meet in a bus stop?"

They giggled, and Cleo answered, "No, we met in a server room."

I snorted. "And what were you doing in the server room? Up to no good? Let me guess, Helena caught you."

"Actually, we caught her." Cat looked smug.

I put my hands up, "Okay, okay, how about from the top?"

The water on my shoulders felt wonderful, and I felt I could stay here for ever. I listened as Cat told me how university had started out for them as normal students. Boyfriends, pubs, evenings out, tutorials. The work had been easy, each enjoying the space of a separate subject, but comparing notes, figuratively and literally, and keeping up with each other's subject interest, just as they seemed to work so well in unison here.

"It's like we can distil information and pass it over without talking too much." Cleo explained, "and we sometimes went to each other's lectures, just to keep up, as well as to make things more interesting."

I smiled at the thought of the poor lecturers being unaware as to which twin was being tutored. I became aware of a pause and I wondered if I had missed a vital cue.

"But, it all went wrong when Creepy Cowdry became besotted with Cleo." I noticed Cleo stiffen ever so slightly beside me. "He was one of her Applied lecturers, and he hit on her." I thought it was safest to continue staring at the floor.

"Actually," Cat continued, "first, he hit on me by mistake, because he didn't know she had a twin and he couldn't tell us apart." I felt slightly sorry for him. "He was boasting about his new car—actually it was an old Porsche but it looked swanky—and trying to get me to come for a ride." Another pause.

"So I made the mistake of telling Cleo—" and here Cat stifled a small sob. I stretched out my arm instinctively to her shoulders, and then had to move it down to avoid the torrent of water. However, the flow didn't diminish as I moved down her back, and then I realised that I wasn't going to find clear water—indeed I was most likely instead to end up in deep water—so I quickly withdraw, honour intact. She pushed into me by way of thanks.

The slight pause had allowed her to recover. "So I told Cleo, and she thought it would be fun, you know, older and everything, so she allowed him to talk her into it. She was eighteen."

"That was taking advantage," I offered gallantly, not feeling at all sorry for him now.

Cat shook her head. "She also knew he had other girls. She

knew it was going to just be a fling, but she didn't care.

"What was taking advantage was that he pushed her; was really mean to her, but that was just the start." I wasn't sure if the water was now reducing the tension in my shoulders or increasing it.

"There was a media lecturer who was into film making. What Cleo didn't know was that they were taking turns filming each other with the girls. Real 16-millimetre movies."

I was shocked. The water pounding was suddenly too much. I asked her to turn mine off. We waited as the cascades quietened, and after a minute she suggested the steam room. The short walk allowed me time to think.

We sat together, like watching a football match, facing the same way, looking through the condensation to the shower room beyond. I looked to my left, to encourage Cat to continue, but the girl looked across me, and I realised I had swapped them again. I tried right.

"So? Did you catch them?"

Cat shook her head. "Cleo had already decided to break up with him. It was just before end-of-year exams and she wanted to spend more time studying. I didn't have a boyfriend at the time, and we were missing each other, so she told him it was over."

This time Cleo sniffed, and I was able to put an arm round her without fear of bottoming out. She responded by resting her head on my shoulder.

"When Cleo went to talk to him and told him it was off, that's when he showed her some of the movies. He said if she left, he would load them on the net. He also called her an ungrateful bitch and hit her right across the face. She came home in a terrible state." I could feel Cleo's silent tears, flowing onto my shoulder. I was helpless, wondering what to do.

Sit. Listen. Some new, wise, personage decided to reveal himself. I stayed sat, but tightened my grip around Cleo's waist. After a while, I prompted, "So what did you do?"

"It was the day before one of her big papers. She was too messed up in her head to go, so I went in her place instead.

"The problem was that the bastard was one of the invigilators. He couldn't figure out how she could be so calm, and it gave me pleasure to see him squirming."

"So you sat her maths exam."

"Yup, one of them, but she sat my biology a few weeks later, so it wasn't really cheating, although, technically it was." I had never heard something so bizarre, but in the midst of all this it seemed almost normal. Then I realised how this might have backfired.

"It was a problem because he figured it out."

"Yup, about a week later he noticed she still had a little cut over her eye from where her hit her, but when he had seen me at the exam the day after, I hadn't had any marks on my face. So, he asked around and found out we were twins.

"He said he was going to report her, us, to the Dean for cheating, but he couldn't exactly use the evidence of her eye without implicating himself, so he flunked her for the paper, even though I got a first for it." Cat allowed herself a bit of pride.

"He told her that to make up to him for not having her thrown out of the faculty, she had to go to Ireland with him for the summer, or he'd upload the films."

"But surely those would implicate him too."

"Well, they were very careful to hide any identifying features of *theirs*. And they could cut out anything that showed too much of them. They knew exactly what they were doing." Cat paused a moment. "We even thought of leaving university."

The way she said 'we' so casually sent shivers down my spine. Helena had called them competent. I now realised that she had understated things. The identical look, the dressing alike; finishing each other's sentences; saying things together. These were just the outer veneer of a much deeper synergy. Together, they would be ... Mr Cautious was suddenly alert. He supplied the word 'dreadful'. Not in an icky way, but in the sense of inspiring dread. Seated as I was, sandwiched between the dreadful alliance, I tried out other words in my head: daunting, intense, indomitable.

Cleo had straightened up, so I let go of her. There was a 'but' coming.

"But?" I supplied, looking at Cat.

"We made a plan to find the films," smiled Cat. "Cleo told him she would go away with him, to buy us some time. Then we started snooping, gathering passwords, 'borrowing' keys and gaining access to all sorts of places, because we knew that the films had to be somewhere on campus where they could share them.

"We got hold of a few little motion cameras and set them up in places where we needed to gather passwords, or to see if a cupboard or room was used. And that's when we first saw Helena. One of our cameras filmed her in the admin reception trying out different passwords.

"When we found out that she worked there, it seemed strange that she should be spying on her own department, and we didn't understand what she was doing. But we did get a few good passwords off her, without her knowing, of course."

The mood was lifting slightly. I was amused that Cleo and Cat were the ones spying on Helena. Cat was sounding quite pleased at their achievements. "Once we had hacked Creepy Cowdry's account we went through all his files. We couldn't find anything useful, but one document had a bit at the end that maybe was an old list of girls names and times, but nothing more. We thought it might be running times of films.

"By now we had access to the server room, and we decided to look for backups to see how old the list was. Cleo had liberated the access card of a young and impressionable network engineer, and we swiped ourselves in, late one evening. We weren't being particularly quiet, and as we opened the door, there was Helena, inside one of the cabinets."

Cleo laughed, this bit she clearly enjoyed, and at last she took on the tale. "By now we knew she wasn't just a receptionist, so when she tried the 'what do you think you're doing in here', we called her bluff. Cat and Helena were like two tigers circling each other while I was still feeling a bit intimidated. It was Helena who suggested maybe we both had good reasons to be there and maybe we didn't need to tell each other what those reasons were."

"But," Cat interrupted, "Cleo broke down at that point and the whole story came out.

Helena stopped us after a while and we went back to her hotel room. It was way too swanky for a receptionist, and she told us about her granddad, and this place, and how she was working undercover as a receptionist because of a student who had gone missing."

Both girls were now looking distinctly nostalgic as they recalled the meeting. I found I was wishing I had been there.

"She fed us room-service steaks and hot chocolate, and then we slept in her bed."

Cleo hesitated. "I mean we did, she was on the floor, and by breakfast we had decided we were friends." She paused again, and I looked each way as they stared ahead, individually reminiscing on the sweetness of the moment. It was the first time I saw them working independently and it was almost more chilling than when they acted in concert.

"And?" They had yet to tie up the loose ends. Cat stretched, ready to get up.

"Helena told us about the missing girl. I recognised her name because it was on the list we found. The next evening we all broke in to the server room together, and with Helena's help, we found the backups, found when the name was added, and it was just before she went missing.

"Then we found a deleted email with the key-code to the gym, which seemed significant. So we set up a few cameras to watch it, and sure enough, Friday evening, we saw both of them go into a storeroom at the back of the gym. The next night, we went in, and Helena picked the lock on the only secured cupboard, and it was full of film, one reel per girl. Some of them were quite long. They used to watch them in the gym conference room."

I waited out the silence that followed. Both girls were lost in the memory. After a suitable pause I prompted:

"And the missing girl?"

Cat looked sad and shook her head. "Never solved. Cops never proved if they were directly responsible, but they got sent down for a long time. They pleaded not guilty, the rats." She didn't say rats. I wasn't sure I'd heard the word, and I'd hate to suggest she knew it. She almost spat it out.

"That must have been hard on you, Cleo? Testifying in court, and everything."

"No." She hung her head, the invoked past still close enough to hurt. I bit my lip in regret at speaking, but she breathed in deep and lifted her chin. "Helena pulled my film before she called the police. She helped me burn it."

Another pause followed before Cleo spoke again, quietly, but completely in control. "We burned the film in his car, in the middle of the university car park, right outside where he was lecturing. When he saw it through the window, he came rushing out and was jumping around trying to put the fire out with his jacket.

"Helena had tipped off the police and they arrived while he was there. He thought the police cars were responding to the fire. She used her phone to film him jumping up and down beside the burning car. She uploaded it onto YouTube. I loved her for that."

I exhaled slowly. It must have been harrowing, but even at

eighteen they were clearly very resolute. I wondered how they had joined the 'family'.

"So you came here after Uni."

"No," said Cat, standing as Cleo did.

They embraced and twirled together. The one facing me through the fog of steam continued, "We came down here for holidays, found we worked well together, and at the start of third year, this was our official address."

I was impressed. I wondered if their gamine looks had made the vote any easier. "And you got voted in okay, like, first time."

"No." said the one furthest from me, "we didn't get voted in."

They opened the door of the steam room and stepped back into the showers, arm in arm, then turned back together and said in one voice:

"We were the first."

My surprise meant that I was nodding absent-mindedly when I realised the right-hand twin had asked, "Do you mind if we ask Marek to join us?" The suggestion didn't help with my thought processes, but my still nodding head had already given assent even before I had processed the question.

Neither made any attempt to summons him, and at the time I didn't know about the messaging capabilities of the not-so-average shower, so I was staring at them a little intently expecting something to happen.

I looked at their slick bodies, seemingly identical in every aspect. And then, in the clearer light of the room, there was a glint right in front of my eyes, a crescent of gold guarding the rosy crest of a perfect little hillock.

I looked across and realised they sported mirror circlets. One of them was smiling; the other biting her lip.

"So now you know which is which," the left-hand angel said.

"And who is who," said the other.

"And how we came to be here," they finished in perfect unison.

I picked up a towel and as I turned back, they were still standing there, but the bands had vanished. I couldn't quite believe it until I realised the little foxes had switched. I wondered how often they managed this stunt when people weren't aware of it.

Marek entered just as I had retreated to the back massager. I had lots to think about, so I left them to him for a while and shut my eyes, allowing the water to lull me into a soporific trance.

***

I don't think I dozed off, but I was suddenly aware that the water was shutting off, and when I opened my eyes there were just two of us left.

"Let's go see if the paint is dry," she said, offering me a hand. I didn't really want to, but she towelled me so nicely I thought it would be rude not to reciprocate. Once we were both dry, I let her take my hand and lead me into the bedroom. The smell of drying paint was a little potent, but undeterred she removed the plastic cover from the king-size bed. Underneath it was a crisp duvet covering a crisper white sheet. She rolled onto her back and, patting the space beside her, invited me to lie down. I hesitated.

"So you two share this room?"

"Yes, but we're seldom here."

I decided to leave it there. Parts of my psychology course were popping up, trying to remind me of the rules of socialisation. I was sure that too many questions were not good manners.

I looked at the girl. Cat or Cleo, I wondered. I can't call you left-hand side, I thought. Mr Grumpy snorted. 'Hand isn't the word you're looking for, stupid.' I blushed.

"What do I call you?" I tried, as I lay down beside her.

"Call me Panther."

“Oh, so you’re Cat.”

“We’re both cats. One of us is a panther, one is a leopard.”

I could find no correlation to their real names, so I gave up. She propped herself on an elbow, leaving her other hand free to trace on my stomach. “Do you know what panthers and leopards do?” she enquired softly. I shook my head, no.

But after while I could answer half of that question.

I remembered a psychology lecture that said an important part of socialisation was learning to take turns, and so I wasn’t watching paint dry the entire time. However, when I was, it turned out to be a lot more interesting than I’d been led to believe.

Much later, my night was punctuated by a dream of Tarzan. Several Tarzans, lots of big cats, clear blue skies with angels that alternately yowled and purred and mewled, and in the middle of it all, a tall lithe Jane that looked remarkably like Helena. But all this just washed over me like waves in the shower, and for the most part, I rested unawares—a sleep of blissful contentment.

20 – Picking Cherries

I awoke feeling distinctly chilly, the duvet down somewhere near my feet. Two of the windows were open, no doubt to let the paint smell out, but without curtains, the overcast morning made the room feel grey.

I reached to pull up the duvet and discovered there was no sign of my feline companion. However, in her place on the bed was a plate with one little croissant on it, and a note in beautiful script saying 'more downstairs'.

I had no choice but to make a dash back to my room in order to find my clothes. Luckily the corridors were clear, and I was soon showered and dressed.

I walked slowly downstairs, savouring thoughts of the night before. The dining room was empty, but the teapot was still warm, and in a large basket covered with a napkin I found more croissants. These were larger, and I wondered if the little one had been made for me especially. I poured myself a mug of tea and sat down with a plate to enjoy a couple with marmalade and butter.

Two helpings later, and thinking of at least one more, I decided to visit the kitchen for some fresh tea. Perhaps I would learn the name of the croissant bearer.

I carried the pot through and was relieved to see a familiar face, or at least a familiar pair of green shoes. Cleo looked up as I entered and leapt to her feet. "James! Darling." She gave me a resounding kiss.

So, I thought, that settles that. I put the teapot down and she turned to put the kettle on. I rested my back against the counter, ready to continue the conversation of last night, when Cat bounded into the room, saw me, changed direction, and snuggled into me all in one lithe movement. "James! Darling." The kiss was uncannily similar.

Now I was back to square one. I looked at her wide innocent eyes, and then across at Cleo—the same expression.

I tried to see if they would solve my dilemma for me.

"Ladies, whichever of you brought me a croissant this morning, and much happiness last night, I thank you."

"You're welcome," they said in perfect unison. I looked at each of them, trying to find some clue, but their faces were equally bright, equally cheerful, and all-together too innocent to be credible. I sighed and gave up, at least for a while.

Cleo poured the water into the teapot, turning it round for me to carry. She also produced a plate with three rashers of bacon on it from out of the oven.

"So you can build your strength up," Cat giggled.

I carried the tea and plate back to the dining room and found Helena sitting there alone, with her iPad propped up in front of her and a croissant in her hand. She was wearing very modest pyjamas. I sat beside her. She smiled at me, sniffed the air, and then stole one of my bits of bacon, sandwiching it in the remains of her croissant.

"Here's an interesting thing," she said, consulting the tablet. "There are reports of the kidnapping of a senior executive of Pharmaply. Some sources are naming Wuthers as the victim." She cocked her head as she re-read this, trying to decide what it meant. "No confirmed details as yet."

She looked up into the distance, reached a decision and, tapping the tablet said, "We'd better have a meeting."

***

Robert had gone to town on business and to collect his old laptop, and Alex was seeing to the pigs so we started with just the six of us.

"There are two things worrying me," Helena started, counting on her fingers. "One, who would kidnap Wuthers and why? Someone apart from Zolotran is obviously interested in their work, and thinks Wuthers knows something.

"Then there is the muscle that 'met' James yesterday, clearly looking for me and the floppy disks.

"Which leads to, two: what *is* going on at Pharmaply?"

She paused a moment, sunk in thought. "I suppose we should add, three: what is Zolotran up to? Xander Street has been a bit coy about exactly what he wants us to find. We normally get more specific instructions as we progress with a case, but he has been somewhat hands-off."

"What's he like, Street?" I asked.

"I haven't met him. Usually we avoid meeting customers," she explained. "They get in touch with us electronically and we operate entirely behind the scenes as far as we can, using pseudonyms and the odd disguise."

"But he has your phone number." I was remembering that rainy night in the bus shelter.

"Correction, he has the number of 'Emma Vaughn', and that's only for this operation." She paused, and after a second I realised it was because I was staring at her fingers, fascinated by the way they made quote marks so eloquently. Our eyes met briefly. I looked down, embarrassed, and she continued. "So, our priorities are: James and Marek, I'd like you to concentrate on network traffic at Pharmaply. Let's get into it and find out what's going on. Start with the easy stuff and let's work from there.

"Robert hasn't had a chance to look at the floppies yet, but he will when he gets back. If he can't, we'll send them out for full forensics.

"Celestine, please do a round robin of our usual contacts. See if we can find out anything about who might have taken Wuthers. And you two," the twin heads turned as one, fixing their eyes on Helena. "Stop that," she said, but she was smiling.

"Cleo and Cat, please could you think of a way to get us a look at the fifth floor at Pharmaply. I'm not convinced it's just building work going on there."

"Inside or outside?" asked Cat. Helena shrugged, either.

"We have a solution, mistress." They adopted a robotic monotone. Helena's eyes widened, not quite believing it.

"You can get in?"

"We can get *out,* if a look through the windows will do," said Cat looking pleased with herself.

"Yes," followed Cleo immediately, "then you can look in as much as you want."

She spent a few seconds on her phone and then produced a photo of a lime-green boom with four wheels at the bottom and a platform at the top.

"Cherry picker."

She began to read. "The HR21 four-by-four self-propelled cherry picker lifts two persons and their tools to a height of 21 metres."

"Won't they notice a big green thing looking in at their windows?" I couldn't contain myself.

Helena looked at me, brows raised to warn me that interrupting the twins would spell trouble.

I turned to them, looking for the slight pause that would suggest I had made a valid point. Instead, they just blinked. I'm sure it was just coincidence, but they did it together. Cat explained first.

"Yes, if you park it outside their door, they will notice. But if you park it across the street in this car park here, then they won't." She indicated a large retail shed on the aerial photo on her phone. No one would ask why, so I started to, but Cleo cut me off.

"Because 'Furniture Life' is having a sale. We just have to copy their promotional material and then we can pitch up with our cherry picker and pretend to be a 'Special Events Unit'. We load up a sign saying 'Sale', and then lift it as high as we want. Marek's camera will do the rest."

I tried one final face-save. "And we have a cherry picker?"

"Oh no," said Cleo.

"We hire one," finished Cat. It was brilliant in its simplicity.

Helena gave her approval to these activities, and Marek

and I set off to his workshop. He patted me good-naturedly on the shoulder as we walked out and said "Never argue with a being that has more brains than you." Were two heads better when they thought like one, I wondered.

***

Once in his office, Marek talked me through what we had set up in the Kombi at Pharmaply the previous evening.

"So, the access point in the van has Wi-Fi access, across the stream, to the server room." He showed me a pair of directional aerials like the ones we had left on site.

"The van is running a small server to collect any data we instruct it to. From here, using mobile data, we have internet access to the van, so we can control its server and make it do searches for us." I nodded, so far so good.

"And we can get live video from the camera if we don't need much other data." He pressed a button and the feed appeared on one of the monitors on his desk. The camera was pointing at the Pharmaply building. He adjusted the field of view and we could see a large truck reversing into one of the loading bays. Next to it an identical white vehicle was already parked.

"Let's see what we've got so far." Marek tapped away at his keyboard. We had left the van collecting standard broadcast traffic to get an idea of the network. There was the usual collection of messages from computers letting other computers know where they were. Printers, faxes, servers, and desktops all posting little discovery messages on their binary equivalent of Facebook.

Marek suggested we log in to the switch and persuade it to send us more data. "There are at least two ways." he said. "Brute force, or, you ask the administrator." He smiled.

"And the administrator just tells you."

"No, you don't ask for the password, you ask for help." He proceeded to demonstrate. "As you know, in any large organisation, computers report on their health using a protocol called SNMP.

"So, I've set up the Wi-Fi router to obtain an IP address from the network. Then I look at the range of IP address used by other machines. See these low numbers, these are probably servers."

He ran a program to do a quick scan of the addresses, and many of them responded with a list of their open ports.

"So, each open port indicates a type of server, Mail, DNS, File system. Let's pick an existing file server here"—he wrote down the address—"and we also find gaps in the numbering—spare addresses." He picked one. "I set our Wi-Fi router to a spare address, and then I broadcast an SNMP message saying 'I'm a computer and I have an error and I need help', and now we wait and see."

We sat and watched the router. A minute later, an administrator, somewhere on the network, responded to the computer's help message and tried to log on to our router. Of course, they didn't know it was ours, they thought it was a Pharmaply server in trouble. Our router asked for his username. He gave it. Apparently he was called 'dave.reynolds'. Then our machine requested his password. He gave that too.

Marek showed me how the router was set up to log into a real file server using these credentials, and then to mirror the conversation back to the admin. While the administrator thought he was talking to a genuine server, our router was in fact relaying the conversation to us.

We watched as he did some standard tests and then decided to reboot the server for good measure. Marek had the router disconnect and we looked at each other. We now had the admin password. It had taken less than three minutes.

***

Dave's password didn't work on the network switch, but it did work on all the servers. Looking at the most recent data, a fair amount of it was concerned with vehicle movement orders.

The vehicle shipping schedule proved to be an easy hack. It allowed anyone logged on with a certain privilege level to monitor and alter shipping movements. Our friend Dave had more than enough privilege. The system showed two trucks currently docked at the loading bays we were watching.

Marek was looking at the truck details. "Hmm, Scania; 44 tonne; a few months old; sequential registration plates. Probably about a hundred grand a pop. Pharmaply must be doing well." He was almost salivating over them, and I remembered watching last night on the camera as the driver had gracefully reversed the massive vehicle into the confined space.

"Let's see if we've understood this protocol correctly," I suggested. So, just for fun I told the system to send the left-hand vehicle to an address in Manchester. At once.

A couple of minutes later, we watched as a driver came out of the side door, carrying a rucksack. He jumped into the cab and pulled carefully away. As soon as the truck was out of view, I told the system to bring it back. It took a few minutes, but then the white hulk reappeared and reversed slowly back into the loading bay.

The body language of the driver as he went back inside suggested this was not the first time the computer had screwed up. We were utterly delighted. Marek suggested maybe we shouldn't tell Helena about these games.

We started digging deeper into their systems.

***

Sometime later, Celestine came in to queue her artwork for printing. Marek offered to babysit the printer as it went through its early morning warm-up while Celestine went to change. He took the time to show me the hoppers to the left of the printer with the various print stock—paper; card; adhesive film—and the RIP unit that allowed him to tweak the colour settings and finish options.

He lightened Celestine's artwork to lift the colours a little, and after a short warm-up, sets of business cards began to print, eighteen to a page. The three sheets of A4 popped out faster than I could walk the length of the machine.

Ten minutes later, once Marek had taught me how to guillotine to crop marks, he left me cutting up the cards while he printed the 'Sale!' banner in the room next door. Soon we had a little pile of fifty cards, the rolled-up banner, and two sets of plastic film proclaiming 'Special Events Unit' with a beautiful furniture logo to match the cards.

Marek carefully extracted a Range Rover from the garage and we decorated it with the newly printed film, turning it into a 'Special Events Unit'. We were just finishing as Helena came out with Celestine and the twins, who were dressed somewhat garishly in pink and purple jumpsuits to match the corporate branding. Celestine was hefting a professional looking video camera. Marek showed me the side lens—while the camera was pointing one way, it could see quite clearly at 90 degrees to the side.

Helena had decided to risk a meeting with Street, so she had a change of clothes in her bag. She asked Cleo to help with her blonde wig and Marek for a tracker to take with her.

I took some test shots through the side lens of the four of them before waving them off, their snug little jumpsuits promising so much more than a perpetual furniture sale.

21 – Takeaways

I spent the day with Marek absorbed in the task of analysing the Pharmaply data streams. Suddenly it was late afternoon and he got a text from Celestine to say they were on their way back with supper. He forwarded it to Robert and Alex.

With me sitting beside him at his desk, Marek typed up a short summary for Helena of what we had found in the Pharmaply data—which wasn't a lot.

So far we knew that a lot of truck movements were being made, with items being carried up and down the country.

Despite our earlier success with the movements schedule, the majority of the endpoints were code words which we did not understand. We thought it possible that in the pharmaceutical business you might not want even your own employees to know where things came from and went to.

Luckily no one had thought to encode the motorway service areas and so from scheduled stops at these, together with overall mileage and time taken, we deduced that that most of the end points were 'up north', probably in the Manchester and Liverpool areas. That was assuming, of course, that the trucks stayed on the main roads.

One useful morsel we did find was that the two trucks currently in the loading bay were due to leave at 9:30 the next day, bound for multiple locations. The route started with both trucks together and then they split.

In his report, Marek outlined a plan to put trackers on the trucks to see where they went to. We were just finishing off, when a skid on the gravel outside announced the arrival of four very hyper young ladies. Helena was dressed in a sober grey suit, but without the wig. The other three looked as though they had had to fight off wild bears.

One of the twins was carrying several large paper bags, and the other, two bottles of champagne, one of which had been opened, and from which she was now swigging. From the little that remained, I surmised that it had been open for a while.

"Cleo's outer split," giggled Champagne girl, pointing to Miss Paper Bag. Sure enough, the seam beside the zip of the jumpsuit had given way, leaving an interesting V-shaped aperture that reached just below her navel.

"Well, it was all we had. I said yours were a bit too small," Celestine muttered, defensively.

"And she got *way* more attention than she should have," Cat bemoaned.

"We all got way more attention than we wanted," corrected Helena. She chivvied them indoors and then turned to give both Marek and me a little kiss each. "Hurry up, it's Indian." We hurried.

***

There is nothing quite like a curry shared with friends; the succulent aromas, the flavours; and the finger-licking tactility of the food. I looked up and caught Robert's eye as he shovelled in a mouthful of sauce on a piece of naan, and he looked positively blissful. I felt the same, although I was using a spoon for the curry.

Twenty minutes later I was replete, but still picking, and on my second beer. Helena asked for a recap of the day.

Marek told of our moderate success on the data stream from Pharmaply, and our suggestion to put trackers on the trucks to see where they went. Helena considered this suggestion, and agreed it was a sensible thing to do. I would need some time to digest before we did another night raid.

Robert cleared his throat. He was looking a little red. He said he had just finished examining the floppy disks Helena had liberated from Pharmaply, and he had found nothing in the files except innocuous data. He showed us the one he had dismantled to look for hidden memory cards but there was nothing inside. The only puzzle was that the data was clearly recent, and it was unusual for a floppy to still be in use, so there had to be a good explanation, but it eluded us.

Helena shook her head.

"I thought they were strange, but I knew they couldn't be used for serious data storage," she said. Her look intensified, becoming a frown.

Celestine was sitting beside Helena, her face lightening the room with its radiance. She had let Helena feed her forkfuls of food, and now she was sitting back, beer in hand. She was happy to let Helena and the twins tell of their joint excursion.

"We arrived a bit early so we could suss out the car park," Cat started. "We found a good spot for the camera at the far end, closest to Pharmaply, and then had to chase off a few shoppers who got too close."

"When the guys with the cherry picker arrived, I was doing some stretches when my jumpsuit split. They were suddenly very keen to help us," continued Cleo, to snorts of laughter from the others as the incident was recalled.

"Of course," Helena continued, "that meant I had to send Cleo and Celestine up into the cherry picker to operate the camera, while Cat and I waited down below."

Helena nodded her thanks to Marek and me: "The banner looked great, wrapped round the cage in the air, and with the camera apparently pointed at the shop below, Celestine got a very good look at that fifth floor." Helena paused dramatically, and turned to Celestine, who simply shook her head, content to let her boss keep going.

"But, first," Helena continued, stringing out the suspense, "once we had finished filming, I went off and met Street. We had a little ride in his MX-3. He asked me if he could have the floppies. I agreed that someone would drop them off tomorrow." She paused for dramatic effect and looked at us. Then the penny dropped.

I said it first: "But you never told him you had any floppies." She was biting her lip, nodding.

"Which is why," she said, "I thought I would leave a tracker under his car door sill as I got out."

"Anyway," Helena said, "while I was off joyriding with Street, the others packed up and looked at the footage Celestine shot. That fifth floor of Pharmaply is no building site. There are lots of desks in the bit we could see, and each one had someone working at it. And," another dramatic pause as her brow smoothed, "there is a new central walled-off bit that isn't on the other floors. And"—she now had our complete attention— "there are two new chimneys that aren't in the satellite picture we looked at yesterday." She finished and looked around. The twins were watching too, to see who would catch up first.

"A lab," Marek said. "It's a new lab. Why do they have a new secret lab, and what are they making in it?"

"Exactly," said Cat.

Further speculation was halted as Robert's little coughs developed into wheezing and choking. Looking at him I could see his cheeks were even redder; his lips were swelling and he was gasping for air. I thought he must have swallowed something the wrong way, but Helena just yelled "EpiPen! Alex, quick!" and then she and Marek were stretching Robert out beside the table.

I sat there, frozen by this rapid activity. Alex was back in seconds brandishing the medicine, her thumb flipping off its lid. Robert winced as she stabbed his thigh muscle. Alex held it and counted before gently pulling back at ten. Robert began to breathe a bit easier.

"What is it?" I asked. The evening had taken a bad turn very quickly.

Helena stroked Robert's head as Cat took bloods. "I don't know. Allergic reaction possibly? It looked like anaphylactic shock. The adrenaline's helping." She was very worried.

We waited ten minutes, then Marek and I helped Robert up to his room.

Cat had already stripped the bed back as we arrived. She

thanked us, and we left her helping Robert undress.

We returned to the dining room. I definitely needed another beer.

Instead, Cleo was making tea. We sat in a sombre group around the now forlorn looking table, sipping tea and awaiting the bike that would collect Robert's samples and take them to the lab. Alex tried to reassure me by telling me about how efficient they were. "If there's anything to find, they will find it." Soon after the bike left, Helena reappeared.

"He's sleeping peacefully. Cat will stay with him. Cleo, you're on standby." The girl nodded. Helena decided we didn't have time to install the trackers that night and instead opted for the morning. "Change of plan, James, we leave at eight. Dress warmly." I nodded, still shocked.

I didn't know Robert at all really, but the thought of losing one of these people was now more than I could bear. The others had drifted off, and so I returned to my room. I showered, and then, feeling miserable, took out my old phone to see if anyone from my old life had called. No one had. The battery was low, so I put it on charge, and went to bed feeling thoroughly alone.

***

I came to, feeling a bit better. I realised most of this good feeling was because I was curled up around a T-shirt-clad girl. From her size I guessed it was one of the twins. It felt very good for a minute or so until the girl woke up and said, "James!" Somewhat abashed, I went to use the bathroom instead. My companion followed, and I had to pretend I found it normal to share facilities like this.

After a minute or so of sitting on the twin thrones with me darting perplexed looks at her, she helpfully said, "Cleo."

"Thank you, I wasn't sure."

"I hope you don't mind?" She looked a little stricken, "it was all so hectic and I had to drive to town and when I got back I didn't want to be alone." I nodded, aware that I had been largely unaware of her presence; she mistook this for bemusement and decided to fill me in.

"After you went to bed, Cat decided Robert should go to hospital. We agreed it was safest if we took him to his office and then called an ambulance from there, rather than have one come here."

I nodded, unsure where Robert's office was located.

"Robert, Marek, and I were on our way, when Helena called to say the lab had asked for more bloods because of some borderline results. So we rushed back here. It was too late to call a bike, so I took the new samples to the lab."

In response to my question as to how Robert was, she assured me he seemed okay but weak, and was back in his room with Cat to keep an eye on him. However, when I asked about why he hadn't gone to hospital she quickly changed the subject by suggesting we shower.

The suggestion seemed to have been made more out of politeness than anything else, as we showered simultaneously, but separately. Cleo seemed to be avoiding contact but was dejected. As we towelled ourselves off, I gave her a hug and told her it would be all right. She gave me a long and searching look before hugging me back, a little perfunctorily, I thought.

We went down for breakfast, but the table was bare, the events of the night before having thrown things off schedule. The whole family, apart from Robert, was in the dining room. They all looked very serious, and I assumed they were worried about their sick friend.

Cat had just finished drawing blood from Marek. Helena asked me if I had felt at all unwell, which I hadn't, and then asked if I minded giving a sample. Or three as it turned out. Helena then did Cleo and Cat. With some solemnity Marek, Cat, and Helena sealed the case. Cleo excused herself and headed for the kitchen.

Helena asked me if I would take a cup of tea to Robert and

sit with him until Cat returned. She picked up the case and, accompanied by Cat and Marek, took it out the front to the waiting bike. I hurried after Cleo to get Robert's tea.

***

I found Robert propped up in bed, reading a book, his glasses a little further down his nose than usual.

He looked pale, but as I knocked and entered, he beckoned me in, a faraway look on his face indicating that he was trying to work something out.

I put his tea on the table beside him, and he thanked me. I told him I had been sent in place of Cat. I sat in the armchair with my own mug.

I'd already noticed that Robert seemed to slow down at times. I had wondered if it was age, but now I got the impression it was just his way of examining things—rather like a big cat who slows before she runs and pounces. I wondered what he wanted, but he brightened suddenly and then said, "Let me tell you how I came to be here." He was watching my reaction closely, and the ensuing silence was a little disconcerting. I could but sit there and alternate my stare between him and the large print of Manet's 'Le Déjeuner sur l'herbe' on wall behind his bed.

He started to speak, each word clear and slow, as though well weighed.

"I met Helena's grandfather, Colonel Fey, when I was just starting out, a junior associate in a small law firm. I was young and idealistic. The world was my oyster. All of my life ahead of me.

"One day, the Colonel came into the office, with Helena in tow. She must have been four or five. He had a patent application and he wanted some advice. I was keen, but I knew nothing about patents, so I promised to find someone who did. He thanked me, and left. The girl looked shyly at me—I was much taken with her, but since I was sending the work away, I didn't expect to see either of them again.

"But before I sent the patent out, I read it and discovered a small mistake the Colonel had made. One that could have affected his rights. I dropped him a note, and he came back in, sans Helena. He was very grateful, and he put in a good word with my boss. And from there, we sort of kept in touch.

"Helena and I crossed paths every few years or so, whenever she happened to accompany her grandfather, and so I saw her from time to time as she grew up.

"I handled her father's estate when he passed. Very sad affair. Very sad indeed." Robert's eyes misted as he recalled events I was not privy to. I wanted to ask, but the tragedy still seemed raw, his eyes were unfocussed, and I didn't want to remind him that I was here.

"Time passed, I inherited the law firm, got involved in the local parish, but nothing else in my life made much progress. I buried myself in work, and tried to ignore any gaps around me." I recognised some similarities between his social life and mine.

"Later, the Colonel wanted to make sure his own estate was in order. He knew he was dying and the last year was rough for him. But he found great strength in this house, in what he had here. Helena was living with him then.

"The Colonel made me promise to make sure she stayed on the straight and narrow—to help her in any way I could. She came in with him just once after that, a very independent young woman. I wondered if she wasn't the girl that could have kept me interested, had I met her twenty years before."

He beamed at this memory, and I remembered my own joy at meeting 'a very independent young woman'.

"So when Helena came to me to ask about the legal aspects of the commune she was starting, I naturally did the best I could. It soon became apparent that a dictatorship was easier to manage than a democracy."

He paused, and I waited for him to explain. His pace was infuriating, but he was fully focused on me again, and I felt unable to hurry him.

"If two people want to live together, then the law is quite straightforward and offers financial protection for one partner if the other decides to leave. And child support, and so on." I nodded in understanding.

"But if you want three or more people to live together, the legal situation is much more complex. At first I tried to find a way to bind them contractually, but I could see numerous issues arising.

"So rather than try and protect them all against each other, I decided to make one the boss—Helena—Madam Dictator." He smiled; I smiled too, the title entirely suited her.

"The others in the commune would merely be like hotel guests. They get paid to work, and part of that pay is deducted for board and lodging. After pocket money, the rest goes into savings, one account per member." He nodded in satisfaction as he recalled his plan.

"Everyone accepts a covenant that sets out with the details; the exclusivity—keeping it in the family"—he smiled—"as well as the terms of who can join and how to leave, and, of course, the penalties that can lead to expulsion, such as breaking the covenant.

"If a member wants to, or has to, leave, then their share of the wealth of the commune is already in their possession. No fuss, no mess." He looked pleased.

"So has anyone left?" He looked less pleased, so I quickly changed this to "I mean, why did you decide to join?"

"Helena offered me a job, looking after the finances and legal stuff. I think she liked the respectability of my C of E leanings. I thought I wouldn't be interested, but Helena can be quite ... persuasive." He was very diplomatic.

"When Cleo and Cat came along, Helena asked me to sort out a few issues with their affairs before they joined. Helena offered me steady work and a ready-made family, and since I'd never really ... settled down, I thought, why not?

"So, I took the oath, with one exception, and I've been very, very happy. They gave me what I was missing, and they keep me young." He smiled again to himself.

I quizzed him about the exception, but he just replied enigmatically, "Lawyers are good at contractual exceptions."

I thought the story was over, but he was still looking at me, watching.

"I sometimes wonder, James, what I would have done if Helena hadn't come along. I wonder if I would have gone off the rails." The gaze was intense now, and I had to break eye contact.

"Are you okay, James? Are there any rails you need help with?" The question was quietly placed in front of me, and then left for inspection. I felt the gap opening for me to say something, but I didn't know what to say. Perhaps he realised I wasn't good at belonging. After a minute of silence, he thoughtfully coughed and then asked me to fetch Cat. As I shut his door, I realised that maybe he hadn't needed a sitter after all.

Downstairs, a breakfast of toast and tea passed in some silence with the occasional significant look. I've always been a bit paranoid, but I felt I was getting more than my fair share of glances.

The trauma of last night lingered and I felt the divide between us.

22 – The Blue North

My mood lifted somewhat after breakfast when I saw how Helena intended to track the trucks from Pharmaply.

She had found a leather jacket of Robert's which was a bit big for me, but fitted well enough over my jumper, and she led me out to the garage where the Veyron brooded on the cobbles outside. Just the sight of the car filled me with excitement, which I tried to damp down since everyone else seemed so muted.

Helena's own outfit would have been more at home on a motorcycle, but the bright yellow leathers lacked safety panels, and the resulting look was very sleek and chic. She opted for her own hair since the top was off.

We jumped in. She passed me her rucksack to put between my feet and placed a black wig between the seats. I saw with some surprise that she was brandishing a knife. "Always travel in a car with a knife, James," she said.

I pointed out it wasn't much use against a gun, but she smiled at me indulgently and said it was to cut seatbelts in case of an accident.

Helena made room in her side compartment by passing me the twin boxes of deactivated trackers that I had left there after Marek and I had figured them out. She said she insisted on a knife being within reach of the driver of every car she had. It seemed a little excessive, but she was the boss, so I just stuffed the tracker boxes into my door and gave a shrug.

"James!" She sounded irritated, and I muttered a sorry.

Helena drove, but treated the beast with some respect. We rolled gently up the avenue, and finally onto the main road. As we left she said, "I'm pretty sure you must have found the right tracker, James, but to be on the safe side, we'll go slow until we can be sure."

After a little pause, she added, "I'm sorry I yelled at you. It's just my daddy was trapped by his seatbelt. If he had had a knife, he would be alive today." I could see something was troubling her, and I figured it wasn't car safety, so I said sorry and told her it was okay.

She kept the speed under thirty until we were nearly in town, pulling over every so often to allow traffic to pass.

Instead of the motorway, she deliberately chose the ring road with its multiple exits, and we circled the north-east corner of the city at various speeds, often slowed by the city traffic. We were on the lookout for any indication that we had not located the final tracker in the car, but nothing untoward happened.

After forty minutes, Helena looked satisfied. As she turned round and headed for the now familiar business park, she explained her plan to follow the trucks as far as we could.

We arrived at Pharmaply a little after 9:15, parking in the next door lot near the furniture store so we could watch unobtrusively. While we stretched our legs, Helena showed me where they had placed the cherry picker yesterday morning. She seemed preoccupied and I noticed she kept glancing my way. I presumed it was something that I had done, but I hoped I was wrong.

Helena called Marek, who was back at the house watching the video feed from the Kombi. At exactly 9:30 he reported that the first of the trucks was setting off. We heard it, and then it appeared around the building and exited onto the road. The second followed less than a hundred metres behind. Helena decided not to follow them immediately since we knew roughly in which direction they would be heading. So it was that a few seconds later we saw a black Range Rover appear and drive off after the truck. Marek was suddenly shouting frantically over the phone.

"Helena, black 4x4, four guys, they've got semis."

Helena let him know we had seen them, hung up, and we set off. Helena looked hunted, and it reminded me of how she had been shot at on the night we had met. I wasn't sure if her worry was me or the guns, or both, but something was definitely wrong.

We caught up with the convoy. The trucks were one behind the other and the Range Rover trailed them by a few hundred metres. We drove carefully, just keeping them in view, but once we hit the motorway Helena hung well back and let the group disappear ahead of her.

To break the silence I remarked how it was fortunate that Alex had had an EpiPen in the house. Helena muttered 'Bees', and I dropped the subject as she seemed focused on the road ahead.

After a while, she asked me, rather abruptly, about my past again, but this time she probed more firmly round the edges. Every aspect I had previously mentioned she seemed anxious to hear again, and if I deviated at all, she asked yet more questions.

I wasn't sure this level of questioning was polite, but I was impressed by her memory for detail. I had the uneasy feeling that some trust issue had arisen, but I couldn't see I had done anything wrong, so I answered her as simply and straightforwardly as I could. Despite the thoroughness of the inquisition, it was good to be able to share myself with her. I wondered when I would get to ask some questions.

My interrogation was interrupted by a sign for the services. I asked if we could make a quick stop. Helena left the motorway and parked a little distance from the entrance. She said she was following me in to pick up some sandwiches but I felt as though she was keeping an eye on me. As I exited the loos, she was standing right there, alert and watchful.

Before we set off again, I wondered about asking her what the problem was. I was trying to frame the question when she told me our stop had changed the plan a little. She asked me to look inside her bag.

"We know they split somewhere ahead, and we can't follow both of them, but, we also know that they're scheduled to pull over sometime, and when they do, we'll stick our own tracker on each of them." She pointed at the devices I had taken from her rucksack. Each box had a thick black magnet glued to one side, and an on/off switch. She looked at me and raised an eyebrow.

Responding to her unasked question, I assured her I could figure out how to activate them. Then I realised the question was 'could I fit them?' Remembering the semi-automatics, I just nodded, trying to convince myself I didn't mind nosing around while the guards were armed.

Helena sat back behind the wheel and we continued. She had me look up all the services on my phone, and then every time we were getting near one, she would speed up the Bugatti until we could see the convoy ahead, and then drop back again if they didn't turn off. Just before the fourth stop, the leading truck indicated it was about to leave the motorway, and she dropped right back again.

"I guess we should trust the schedule." She looked happy, and I took it that she was pleased with Marek's and my detective work. Her cheerfulness didn't last long, and as she explained how I would fit the trackers, I kept hoping she might think of something that would make her smile again.

As we turned off, she had me take the wheel while she fixed her wig. I noticed she definitely looked sexier now, but I also realised that I preferred the simpler girl underneath.

As we entered the car park she stopped. I got out with the two trackers and started for the truck side and she went and parked.

It was a relief to be away from the cooped-up tension of the car, and I slowed a bit to enjoy a saunter across the tarmac.

"Look like you're meant to be here," an inner voice prompted. I nodded as I remembered Helena's advice from before. It was her voice, and I was amazed that Messrs Logical, Cautious, and Grumpy were happy to make way for her like this. Pondering the meaning of that took my mind off my destination—and the armed guards.

The lorry park was full enough to provide some cover. Away from the other vehicles, I could see the two trucks parked together, with the Range Rover beside them. Two men were pacing agitatedly around the empty tarmac. There was no sign of weapons, but nevertheless they managed to give the impression they were not to be messed with. I found a good spot behind some shrubbery, and phoned Helena with the okay. Her snort suggested she thought I had taken my time.

I heard the roar of the Bugatti as Helena accelerated back into the lorry park, coming to a screaming standstill on the far side of the trucks. She eased herself out of the beautiful car, each movement exaggerated. The tight leathers hugged her body and, with the front zipper of the top undone all the way to her belly, she guaranteed that all eyes were on her, transfixed.

I was not meant to be transfixed, and it was with some difficulty that I tore my eyes off her, and focused on the trucks. I simply walked out from my place behind the scrubby hedge and slipped under the first truck, and then under the second. Beneath each, I switched on the tracker, letting the magnet attach itself to the steelwork. It took only seconds, then I walked away slowly, without looking back.

When I got to the fuel stop five minutes later, I waited inside as instructed, examining the eclectic assortment of magazines that someone, somewhere, selects as suitable for a petrol station.

A few minutes after that, the Bugatti gently eased in, and I went out and topped up the tank for Helena. We then drove off most sedately, back into the car park, Helena checking her mirrors to see if we were being followed. Once she was satisfied we were not, we pulled up out of the way where we could see the exit. Helena showed me the app to track the trucks, and we watched the stationary blips on my phone while we waited for them to finish their rest stop.

The dots began to move and we watched the twin trucks and their escort drive slowly back onto the motorway. Helena followed at a distance. Sadly she felt the need to do up her zip, giving me a stare as she did so that informed me that she had seen me looking.

Helena let them get about half a mile ahead of us and then she drove at a steady sixty-five, while I kept them in view on the screen.

The trucks separated at the A556, one turned north towards Altrincham, but we stayed on the M6 and Helena risked getting a bit closer to see which way the firepower had gone. We closed the distance to the blip and when the white truck appeared, there was no sign of the 4x4.

I agreed with Helena that the more interesting truck would have the bodyguard, so we decided to abandon this chase, and go after the other one instead. After a quick phone call with Marek, we left at the M56. Helena opened up the throttle and let the road fly beneath us, settling at a steady ton until we reached the A56 turning. The blip on the app showed that the truck, having only had to do one side of the triangle, was just ahead of us. Sitting behind them was the 4x4. The joy of the drive had lifted me, dispelling both my apprehension and Helena's—she grinned, a little girl freed for a moment of delight.

The phone rang with Marek reporting that the other truck had arrived at what he deduced from a street-view to be a chemical store. The schedule said barrels were being unloaded. Helena asked him to keep an eye on where it went next.

Our truck entered a Manchester industrial estate and drew up outside a ropey looking warehouse. Once we had ascertained that they weren't going anywhere, Helena hid the Veyron round a corner, and dug out another change of clothes.

She wore dark overalls, but this time they looked quite used. I had a flat cloth hat in a similar material, while Helena finished her outfit with a deep-navy woollen beanie.

Once attired, we walked round the other factory-like buildings until we could see the warehouse again. The truck driver had stayed in his cab, as had the men in the Range Rover. We hunched down behind a couple of red wheelie bins to wait too.

Twenty minutes later, when my lower legs were getting cramped, a white Transit van pulled up, and three men got out. They looked around carefully as the others from the Range Rover joined them. There was a short discussion and more looking around.

Seemingly satisfied, the truck was reversed up to the warehouse and one of the Transit men lifted the shutter. Two of our guards entered carefully, their weapons barely concealed as they took up positions just inside the opening door. Watching from our viewpoint we saw them manhandle large blue plastic barrels onto the lorry's tail lift and into the store.

More interesting were two smaller white barrels, the size of waste paper bins, that were carried over to the Transit. Helena took as many pictures as she could, and the whole thing was over in less than fifteen minutes. There was a bit of back slapping and nodding at each other, and then the vehicles pulled away.

We waited for a few minutes to make sure everyone had gone, then I stood up to stretch my aching legs.

Helena's phone rang. There were a few terse words, but then she relaxed. She asked them to say it all again. This time she smiled at me. Again, it felt like I'd done something, but this time good. I definitely preferred the smiley version of Helena. She hung up, looking pleased.

I suggested we try to break into the warehouse, but she

shook her head and pointed at a CCTV camera I had missed. "Besides, I suspect that what we are interested in was what was loaded into the Transit," she said.

I was impressed and I asked her how she knew that; she just smiled and then hugged me.

"I owe you an apology, James Glass. After what happened last night, and with Street asking about the floppies, I did wonder if we had a viper in the nest."

I smiled, uncertainly. "What happened last night?"

She laughed. "Last night we found out the one thing it seems Robert is allergic to. Well, the allergy has only just been confirmed. Last night, all we knew was that he had taken amphetamines." She looked at me. It took me a moment to catch up with her.

"And you thought *I* gave them to him?"

"Well, the thing is," she looked uncomfortable, "your first test results also had traces of amphetamines, which we discounted because in an early test you can sometimes get false positives. Last night, the lab found traces of exactly the same amphetamine in Robert, and then later they found the antibodies which told us he could be allergic to them.

"That is why we tested everyone again this morning and the results have just come back. You have a diminishing trace, and everyone else is clear, except Robert. Therefore the exposure was recent, and since it was the same drug profile, it made sense that you and Robert were picking it up from the same place." She gave me that enquiring look that asked if I was keeping up.

"And that place is?" I tried hard to think.

"The floppy disks," she finished for me. "I got suspicious about the disks when Robert said all he had done since lunch was work on the floppies. Then I remembered you had played with them just before we took your bloods." I nodded. "Inside each floppy is a white towel stuff and it was loaded with class 'A' amphetamine. You said you'd looked inside one, and must have got a very small dose by opening the shutter. Robert actually dismantled one just before supper. It took a while to absorb through his skin, but handling it at the dinner table and eating with his fingers probably gave him a higher dosage."

I remembered the white inserts, designed to stop the disk from scratching as it rotated.

"But why?" I asked; it was a strange place to carry drugs.

"I don't know. Either Pharmaply are making the floppies, and hence the drugs, or maybe they received them as samples? I reckon whichever way they were travelling they *were* samples, neatly disguised as business data. And given what we've just seen here, I would say that Pharmaply is doing the making—that's probably what was in the two white barrels."

"But what about all the other stuff they've just loaded into the warehouse? That looked dodgy too."

She agreed, "But it can't all be amphetamines. The lab at Pharmaply is way too small for that many barrels of high class drugs."

"Breaking Bad," I joked.

"Or worse," she muttered, putting her arm through mine as we walked back to the car. Her frown was back.

The drive home took much less time, and I was grateful for my overalls under the leather coat. When we got back I offered to burn Helena's leathers for her and got a sharp reprimand for being too clever. "It was just surveillance," she said.

I could tell that she felt she owed me an apology.

23 – Drugs and Other Love

I awoke the next morning refreshed, and at peace with the world. A large part of that world lay beside me, snoring gently. I had learned a lot in the past few hours about the art of a proper apology and I was half-wondering whom I could apologise to in order to improve my skills, when the girl beside me awoke, and swore.

"Good morning, sweet Helena," I chimed.

"We're late for breakfast you big mammoth."

Perhaps she should try the other side of the bed, I thought.

She grabbed her phone, and I was sad that she had to engage in work so quickly.

Half a minute later, she put it down. "Right, meeting postponed for forty-five minutes. Come on, time for a shower and you can wash my back."

Remembering my first shower, I didn't wait to be asked twice, and afterwards there was still time for her to apologise all over again, and so when we finally went downstairs to snatch a bacon bagel, she was most comprehensively forgiven.

Breakfast in hand, we headed to the briefing room. Everyone except Robert was there, and I got an enthusiastic kiss from Alex.

"I knew it couldn't be you," she murmured in my ear. I gave her a hug and sat down next to her. I offered her a bite of my bagel, but she shook her head. A hint of floral perfume wafted over from her, and I had to stop myself from snuggling closer and taking a deeper breath.

Already up on the monitors were Helena's photos of the warehouse and the white Transit. She told the ensemble her theory about the amphetamines.

Marek brought up street-view pictures of the chemical supplier the other truck had called at. Then shots of a medical incinerator facility which had been its second port of call. He suggested they had dumped their waste at this point.

Next he showed the tracker route the two trucks had followed when empty—both had moved on to Leeds. More street-views of another chemical supplier there. Then the route back to Pharmaply's research centre.

Marek told us he had now decoded the driver schedule and showed how the overnight trip back was done by fresh drivers picked up in Leeds.

"I'm confident we can now pretty much see and alter any part of the trucking and driver schedule," he said, "but we don't know all the place codes.

"However, the four stops visited yesterday account for the majority of the weekly traffic." He pointed at a stylised jeep on the screen. "This little icon here is called 'support' which is just a fancy name for the Range Rover used by the guards. Apparently even they get scheduled."

Marek pulled up more diagrams. "Using the Wi-Fi link to the Kombi, we can also now see and interact with the major building systems, alarms, and employee schedules. I'm not sure exactly which employees work on the fifth floor, since nearly half the people in the building are down as researchers, biochemists, or admin assistants."

Then he showed us a recording from the Kombi feed: images of trucks unloading yet more barrels. A further two brand-new trucks were waiting patiently.

"That's a lot of barrels moving around," Helena mused.

"Perhaps it's to put people off the scent," Marek offered. "Lots of barrels in, lots of barrels out, a few important ones hidden in the middle. Apart from the waste, though, we're still clueless as to the contents."

Next up was a map of Xander Street's movements, starting from when Helena had activated the tracker she had slipped under his car. Marek pointed at key spots on the map with accompanying photos. "This is his office; this is his gym; this is his house, wife, two kids, nice garden." He paused, bought up a picture of another, smaller house. "And this is the house where he 'worked late' last night, and here he is at the golf course this morning."

Helena looked at the array of pictures, her forehead furrowing.

"And," Marek concluded, "here's the news article that says that Bill Wuthers wasn't kidnapped after all, apparently he just lost his phone while he was out of town." Helena did one of her snorts.

"It can't be that simple," Helena said. "All those people on the fifth floor couldn't keep quiet about an illicit drug ring. Drugs must be at the centre of this, but how is Wuthers keeping everything under wraps?" No one answered, and Helena frowned and then started to make decisions.

Alex and I were to go out to the Kombi and change over the batteries that were supplying power to the surveillance systems. Marek would continue working on the data stream; Cat and Cleo were to look after Robert and the house while Celestine was to continue trawling our contacts for any sniff of what might be going on. Especially in Manchester.

I noticed Helena didn't give herself any tasks.

***

After a cup of tea, Marek helped me load the four massive lead-acid batteries into the van and then Alex and I donned boiler suits and caps and set off. She let me drive, but asked that I take the corners gently so she did not get carsick. I jokingly said she must have been driving too much with Helena, and she gave an almost sharp reply.

"Helena's a very good driver."

I back-tracked at once. "I'm sorry, I didn't mean to be rude, I'm just saying she's extraordinary and likes driving fast."

Alex's tone softened. "She is extraordinary. And she does drive fast. Gets that from her father."

I felt down into the driver's side door and, sure enough, found a folding knife exactly like the one I had seen stashed in the Bugatti. I showed it to Alex.

"She told you, then," she said.

"She said a knife might have saved him." I expected a nod at least, but Alex was staring ahead, lost in thought.

"James, I think I should tell you something," she trailed off.

I could see she was wrestling with whatever it was, so I gave her time to think, hoping I would learn something more about our secretive boss.

We turned out of the drive; I took the corner carefully as instructed. Alex pointed back at the house.

"This place belonged to Helena's grandfather, the late Colonel Fey." I nodded.

She paused, deciding on which details to share. I sensed reluctance, so I held back, and even lifted my foot off the accelerator a little to help her find her pace.

"I first came to work for him as a gardener when I was just sixteen.

"I wasn't much good at school.

"Bright, but not interested."

These sentences trickled out. I sensed they were not really what she was trying to say, but she needed to find a starting point, so I remained patient, letting the quiet rhythm of the engine soothe me, hoping the lull would entice her to talk.

"And there was some trouble with the police.

"Working for the Colonel was like community service." I nodded again, to encourage her, while trying to map out in my head where she was going with this.

Alex was looking out of her window, holding her head rigidly. I drove a mile in silence, until, with a sigh, she turned her head back to stare out of the windscreen. I concentrated carefully on the road as she started to speak.

"At first I resented him and his big house and all his cars, and the way he talked so proudly of his wonderful Air Force son who had a perfect wife and perfect child, and how they lived in perfect houses near perfect air bases." She regressed with the memory, the hurt showing plainly on her face, her voice sounding younger.

We entered a bit of road where the oaks were taller, more majestic, patient. She took a deep breath, and I thought she relaxed a little.

"The Colonel worked for military intelligence, but I didn't find that out till later. I was just so angry, and so selfish, and so hurtful and—he saved me."

I wondered if trees felt such pain as was in her voice; whether patience and steadfastness were enough to overcome anything.

"James, I'm telling you this because"—she lost her courage for a moment, then pressed on—"because when we thought you were on drugs, I remembered the bad things of my own past, and I felt so terrible that no one had come to save you, as I had been saved."

That gave me something to think about. I almost didn't hear Alex as she continued.

"That night, when the results came, Helena nearly broke the covenant for you."

I looked at her in amazement. She caught my eye and nodded. "She was prepared to lose all this"—she waved at the valley—"if she could save you. Everyone understood, and no one tried to stop her. It was terrible. And, you see, for me, it was like déjà vu."

She paused and caught a short breath. I turned to see tears forming in her eyes. I looked straight ahead. Another mile passed in silence before I dared to look again. The tears were streaming silently down her face.

Now I started to understand her internal struggle. This was deeply personal. I wished I had a handkerchief or something to pass her. I considered stopping, but with the busy road it would have made it worse, so I gave her space and let her take her time. After a while she started again, in a slightly different place.

"The Colonel was divorced, and I didn't see, that in his loneliness, he found some solace in his cars. I just thought he cared more about them than anything else."

Again there was silence, and then she gave a slight lift of her chin as she breathed in, and was transported back in the memory.

"He had a Blue Ford Model A. It was the most beautiful thing I had ever seen, and it was his pride and joy. I used to have to clean the cars on a rota, and whenever it was the turn of the Model A, he used to come and watch. And as I would start to dry it off, he would come and take the leather out of my hand, and say, 'Here, like this.'"

She smiled, the love and pain combined on her face. "It wasn't that I didn't know how, or that he didn't want me to dry it, he just wanted to feel her under his hand, to see the ancient paintwork start to gleam again. He used to say that it wasn't the most expensive car he owned, but it was the one he most loved."

The road passed almost serenely below us, but in the car I sensed her tension. It didn't seem that this story was going to end well for her. I wondered why Alex would want to tell it to me. I could only wait, tension stiffening my own shoulders.

And then as she spoke again, the banks of self-control broke, and in a rush it all came out, an unstoppable torrent.

"Maybe it was the word 'love' that pushed me over the edge, because one afternoon when he was out, I took a knife from the kitchen and I went to that car and I slashed the upholstery over and over, like I was stabbing someone. I just couldn't stand the beauty of it; the perfection of his life; the way he loved it while I had been abandoned by my family, never quite making the grade. Left in the middle of nowhere, where no one cared." She trailed off.

I empathised with her pain—the never quite being in the right place at the right time. That had been the story of my life to date. Until the bus shelter, when the world had shifted. Again I strained to hear her as she resumed the story.

"And then I ran. I didn't get further than the woods. I loved it there. I realised that despite the anger, his place had become the only place I ever knew as home. I knew that what I had done to him was unforgivable, and I knew I was never going to be allowed back, so I sat there and I cried and cried for everything I had lost, everything I had thrown away without even realising that I had ever had it."

I could see her heaving shoulders and my heart reached out to her. I remembered the word Helena had used about me: lost. But I had never felt as lost as this. I had to stare at the road ahead, blinking hard. She sobbed. I waited patiently; let her pull herself together before she continued, her words a bit calmer.

"It was late afternoon when he found me. I expected him to have the police with him, but he didn't.

"He said he wanted me to come to the East Field. I was old enough to know what that could mean, but I thought I might be able to buy my way out of it, and by then I was willing to do anything to stay, so I went, prepared to give myself rather than leave the only place I could call home. But it was far worse than that."

I remembered myself at that age, vulnerable. I dreaded where this story might go, but I couldn't stop her.

"He had parked the Model A in the middle of the field. On the ground beside it was polish and a cloth. He had buffed her up after he had driven her there so she was gleaming in the evening sun.

"I had made such a mess of the upholstery, that he had to put a cushion on the front seat to drive. And then—" she was sobbing helplessly now as she recalled the events "—And then, he took a tin of petrol. Even the tin was old and well polished, and he took the lid off it and emptied it all over the car, and in the car. Then he took matches out of his pocket, gave them to me and said, ‘Go on, light it’.

“I refused. I didn’t understand what he was doing. So he lit a match and touched the bonnet and the car just blazed up. He told me to stand back. At first I threw myself at the flames to try and put them out, but in seconds the heat drove me back.

“He was walking away, I think he couldn’t bear to look at the car and I remember running after him screaming, ‘Why? Why?’ and finally he stopped and turned, just as the tank exploded.” She sobbed more quietly now. I thought the worst might be over. She took a deep breath and looked across. I kept my eyes firmly on the road.

“James, I will never forget what he said to me. He said, ‘Alex, I loved that car more than anything I own. But if I had to make a choice between losing that car and losing someone, then I would lose the car and chose the someone. I lost my wife because I didn’t care enough. I hope I now might be able to keep a gardener.’”

She gave one more sob, wiping her eyes on her overalls. Then she sniffed. The mood lightened as she composed herself.

“These aren’t tears of pain, James. I’m sorry if I’ve embarrassed you, but I once thought life was hopeless and then someone, he, showed me I had some worth.”

I remembered Helena showing me that she thought me of value, and my heart warmed to Alex for sharing something so deep.

“A few weeks later, he was going to have the burnt wreck taken away, but I asked him to leave it where it was. As a reminder to both of us, and he cried then too. It’s still there. I must show you some time. A mark of respect.”

I thought it was a remarkable story, but there was more.

Alex wiped her eyes again.

“He paid for a tutor to get me some O-levels, and when I turned out to be quite good, he made me do A-levels and then sent me away to university. I didn't know what to do, so he suggested engineering, and for the first time in my life I felt free.

"I stayed away a lot at first, while at university. There were boys and drinking and I did both a bit too well, but I got a good second.

"It was Easter of my final year when I came back to see him. I had spent all my allowance and I didn't have anywhere else to go."

She smiled, and her face glowed.

"That's when I met Helena. She was just ten, with a cute little Scottish accent. She used to stay with the Colonel quite often, but we'd never been there at the same time before."

Her voice dropped again, and I struggled to hear the words as they again became more staccato.

"Her mum had run off with some army bloke.

"I never met her dad.

"Squadron Leader Hector Fey.

"Helena was there because he had just got himself killed in a rally race.

"Swerved off the road into a lake. Coroner decided his seat harness got jammed, and he couldn't get out."

Well, that explained the knife kept close at hand in each car.

"The Colonel asked me to stay and look after his granddaughter, so I did. I swotted for my finals in the morning, and in the afternoon, we would go for walks and I showed her the bits of the woods I loved. She was good with her hands, so to take her mind off things, I suggested we build a pigsty, and then we got our first pig, a saddleback.

"She wanted to call him Elise, after her mum, but I suggested that 'Dinner' would be a better bet, and bless her, she got it, and when the time came later that year, whenever we had pork, she would always say, 'thank you, Dinner, for dinner!'"

I smiled at that. I remembered Helena that first morning saying thank you to breakfast. "And Breakfast."

She looked surprised that I knew. "Yes, the first Breakfast was a Tamworth, we got him soon after, to keep Dinner company." She paused, and I thought she was plucking up a bit more courage. I concentrated on the road.

"And it was after one of those pork dinners that I decided the Colonel and I didn't need to be so lonely any more." I looked over in surprise. She was smiling, the tears drying but her eyes still puffy. We were entering the outskirts of the city, and I felt the familiar depression start to settle on me.

"So, the Colonel? ..." I tried to make it sound gentle, but it wasn't.

"Cancer. He died just after Helena finished uni. She didn't know, but he couldn't hide it from me." There was another wistful pause.

"He left the house to Helena. She had grown up tinkering in the garage and the workshop and playing with all the surplus military kit he had gathered over the years.

"After he retired, he did private security stuff, and she'd helped him in some projects, so she knew her way around.

"And he gave me the right to live in the house as long as I wanted."

I was growing used to the pauses now, and so I tried to relax, shaking off the weight of city driving, letting her words flow unimpeded.

"After Helena met the twins, they started coming over more and more frequently." I nodded; I knew this bit. "Then one day she said to me, 'Alex, if there's anything I learned from my father and my grandfather it's that the Feys have always been bad at keeping their women. I think we need a fresh start.'

"I was amused by the 'we', but I listened to Helena's ideas for the commune. I told her I thought I was too old for some hippy experiment, but I helped her with the basic rules of the covenant—the rights, the obligations, the voting—before Robert got involved. She invited the twins to join her."

Alex sat up as we turned into the industrial estate.

"I continued working in the garden, and a year later, I asked to join. They had Marek and Robert by then, and the twins teased me mercilessly, which was all the worse because I knew what they were voting on. So, since then, I've done my bit in the garden, and polished cars," and here her smile widened.

She seemed much brighter, at ease with herself, accepting the worth she had been given, accepting the pain she carried, not because it hurt, but because it was the story of love. I wondered if I could ever feel as deep or dignified.

We pulled up to the grey Kombi, and she removed a battery effortlessly, while I found them quite heavy. We swapped them in pairs, so as to not disturb the inverter.

"I had wondered who had put in all the elbow-grease on the cars," I said as we lugged lead. "It's a real labour of love."

"Not really," she replied, suddenly bashful. "They're mine. The silly blighter left them all to me."

Now I smiled too, the city gloom lifted, and fresh tears welled up in her eyes.

"I had assumed they were all Helena's."

"Oh, well, many in the garage are. Especially these new-fangled things." She slapped the Kombi as she spoke. "I sold a few of his, mine, to make some room and to pay for improvements to the house, but he'd left her lots of dosh too. Not sure where it all came from." She tapped the side of her nose conspiratorially, found a tear and rubbed her face with her sleeve.

We finished moving the batteries, and I called Marek to check he was happy with the status of the Kombi.

Before we climbed back into our van, Alex said, "Thank you for listening." I went to give her a hug, and she gave me a really nice kiss. I told her there was no charge for listening, and she giggled, suddenly young again.

"The kiss wasn't for listening. That was for fixing Helena's Bugatti. The girl's been nuts about it since she was first given it, and I was so sad she couldn't use it."

Alex turned the radio on as we left, catching the end of Woman's Hour. I felt wonderful as we left the city behind us—our shared silence cementing the companionship that comes of shared sorrow. I didn't hold back on the accelerator now.

***

We parked on the gravel behind the house, and Alex asked if I would help her clean out the hot tub before the weekend. I promised I would. I left her in the garden and entered the house via the back door closest to the kitchen. I was looking for Helena.

There was no one in sight. I entered the dining room and to my surprise saw Robert sitting in his usual spot at the long edge of the table. His laptop lay slightly to his left, unopened.

"You're up," I observed, somewhat redundantly.

"Yes, much better, thank you." He looked a little nonplussed. I wondered if he was hoping for an early lunch, or maybe a late breakfast.

"Are you hungry? Would you like me to go and rustle up Cat or Cleo?"

"Oh, thank you," he replied, "but no thanks, Cat is attending to me."

"See you later then." I turned and left.

I realised how much better I had got at not staring. I had managed to look him in the eye the whole time, and he had managed the entire, if short, conversation without blinking.

If it hadn't been for a single errant pink plimsoll, half-hidden by the tablecloth, I would have been none the wiser. He must be getting better, I thought.

***

With no sign of Helena, I went to my room and saw I had a

message on my old phone. That was a surprise.

It was from Leon, which was less of a surprise, reminding me I owed him thirty pounds for internet café usage. I sighed and pocketed the phone. Leon would have to wait for a few days.

I wondered if I should hate what had been the first twenty-eight years of my life, but Mr Logical stepped in and reminded me that I was the product of my experience so far, and rather than regret the old, I had better jolly well look after the new. I decided it was good advice.

My pocket chimed, and after resolving the confusion generated by being a two-phone owner, I saw it was the house phone, inviting me to a meeting in the briefing room. I hadn't thought to look for Helena there, and set off at a trot. Someone else wanted me too, and I didn't owe them money. I felt very content.

24 – Pack up Your Troubles

I met Cleo and Cat at the door of the briefing room, and, apart from Robert, whom Cat said was resting in the drawing room, we were all there. The atmosphere was lighter, but I perceived that all the upheavals of the past few days had left everyone slightly on edge. I felt nervous too, and my personal advisers, after a leave of absence, were itching to join in.

Helena was sitting on the edge of a table, looking comfortable in some denim dungarees and sandals. She looked up once she realised we were all there and pursed her lips, a little unsure where to begin. She started with the small stuff.

"Marek and Cleo, after lunch I want you to go and see Street at Zolotran. Take him the floppies. If he notices one is missing, shrug and say that is all of them. Don't answer lots of questions; I'll talk to him once we've got some answers.

"Oh, and I'm not happy with all this meeting clients stuff, so please don't make yourselves too describable."

She stared at the floor a moment, before continuing.

"Which brings us to: what we know so far and what is going on?

"We know there's amphetamines involved, but there must be nearly a hundred people working on that fifth floor, and there is no way that Wuthers could hide a secret so big in such plain sight. You simply can't make and ship out barrels and barrels of drugs each week without someone noticing and alerting the authorities."

"They may not be full," Alex put in.

Helena considered this. "You're right, the best way to transport stuff would be to put the drugs in the bottom of a barrel and fill it up with something innocuous. But, still, the armed guards only seemed interested in the two barrels transferred to the Transit, so maybe that's the drugs and everything else is a ruse."

More staring at the floor, and then she reached a decision. "I have to go back in there."

To Pharmaply? I thought she was mad. Then she looked at me.

"James, please would you come with me?"

The plea, even though touching on a command, was heart-warming. I took Mr Logical's advice and said, "Of course, no problem." Mr Cautious was beside himself. I realised the literal aspect of this and laughed. Helena glared at me.

"Celestine, would you monitor the surveillance equipment and let us know of anything untoward?" Celestine nodded her agreement.

"Lunch." Helena's gaze left mine and turned to Cleo, eyebrows raised. Cleo said it was ready. Everyone followed her out of the room and trooped across the hall. As I left, Helena handed me a pair of binoculars to take with us.

We sat down to tomato soup with the twins' wonderful fresh bread. Even Robert joined us, saying he was as right as rain.

The meal eaten, I changed into a shirt, tie, and jacket to re-create my *Nicholas Jones, Pharma Inspector* role. Helena re-applied my tattoo, but using a damp sponge this time, much to my disappointment. She was dressed again in a tight suit and the blonde wig. I was allowed to drive the Golf. We set off behind Marek and Cleo, and they peeled off when we got near town.

I pulled up at the edge of the Pharmaply car park and Helena went through the plan again. I drove a bit further in and dropped her off at a spot that gave me a good view of the reception area through the binoculars. She went in, and I used my phone to log into the surveillance tools in the Kombi, and from there into the building's control systems.

I watched as Helena approached the desk. Miss Passive-Aggressive nodded and escorted her through security, before returning to reception. Helena's phone signalled briefly letting me know she was entering the elevator, I counted slowly to five and then I told the building it was on fire, on the fifth floor.

Within seconds the alarms sounded, and soon people began to stream out of the fire escapes. The plan was for Helena to take the lift as high as she could, hide and then take the stairs to the fifth floor. The lift tried to obey its programming and return to the ground as the alarm went off, but I told it that Helena was a fireman, and it happily believed me. I noted she stopped at the fourth floor. I could see her red dot moving around slowly on my phone. I watched her move about for ten minutes.

My phone beeped.

"Hi, Marek."

"James, where's Helena?"

"She's inside." His tone worried me.

"We're at Zolotran. Street's not here. Celestine says his car is at Pharmaply."

The implications dawned. If Street was here, our world was about to crash. "I've already messaged her," Marek said frantically, "but she didn't reply."

I looked at the phone. The red dot wasn't moving. And then, as I gazed, the dot disappeared. Helena's phone had been disabled.

I could hear Marek voice yelling at me; I put the phone back to my ear.

"I'm here," I said.

"James—" his voice was deadly serious "—just get out. Drive out of the car park and wait for us. These people are dangerous and they have guns. James, do you understand me? Do it now."

I looked up. Two heavies had come out of the building and were walking right towards the Golf. I recognised them from my flat, Mr Large and Mr Little. They didn't look happy. More precisely, their right hands were inside their jackets. I told

Marek I understood, started the Golf and took off with a squeal of tyres.

I didn't go far. I stopped just outside the gate, out of sight and looked back. The goons hadn't follow me.

I put the car back in gear and quietly did a U-turn. I drove past the crowds of employees starting to file back into the building and parked as close as I could to the front entrance.

I opened the door of the Golf, heard the clunk of the knife in the door pocket. It wasn't much use against guns, I reminded myself, but it was better than nothing. I grabbed it, slipped it into my pocket beside my phone. After a quick rethink, I decided to slip the blade into my sock. Remembering Helena's phone disappearing, I transferred my house phone to my other sock as a precaution and ran into the building.

"I'd like to see Mr Bill Wuthers, please," I told the slightly startled Dawn. She phoned and asked me to wait. This time it was not twenty minutes.

As 'Bill' appeared, every instinct I had was telling me to run, but my new-found life was somewhere in this building, and after the near-miss with Robert, I wasn't going to abandon it.

Wuthers' smile could have frozen a small planet. "Come on up. Mr Jones, isn't it?" He didn't offer to shake hands.

The silence in the lift increased my sense of dread, and my worst fears were realised as the doors slid back to reveal the open-plan office of the fifth floor.

I gave a nod to Little and Large who were standing to one side of the elevator, sidearms drawn.

Four men dressed in black and armed with short sub-machine guns stood facing Helena. Her wrists were bound behind her with yellow wire. I recognised the RJ45 connectors of a network patch cable. I couldn't see her from the waist down, because she was standing in a blue plastic barrel.

She had turned as the lift doors opened and looked right at

me. Her eyes told me she thought I was a complete idiot, and I adored her for thinking that.

Standing beyond the goons, looking menacingly at Helena, was Xander Street. He looked even more smarmy than in the photo I had seen in the briefing room.

"So, Miss Vaughn, I take it this is one of your associates?" he asked her.

Wuthers replied, "He also pretended to work for the Department."

Street nodded. "I think we need another barrel," he addressed Mr Large. Large nodded at Little and the two of them moved into the lift.

"Search him." Street instructed Wuthers, who then patted me down. When he felt my old phone, he put out his hand, and I made a show of reluctance before I gave it to him. He passed it to Street, who was holding a small steel cash box. He opened it and put my phone in, next to Helena's. The lid clicked shut. He didn't bother to lock it, but I knew the metal would shield the signal, preventing Marek from seeing us. 'Seeing *her*,' Mr Logical corrected. It felt good to have him around.

Street smiled. It was a thin, nasty, smile. "Your phones will be going south. You, however, will not. If anyone comes here looking for you, then we will simply deny it. If they look at the CCTV, we will say that you said you were government inspectors. If you turn out not to be, who knows what nefarious things you got up to, or where you went to next."

I glared at him, "What's with the 'we' all of a sudden? I thought you were competitors." I was trying hard to think of a rescue plan. Street sneered.

"This morning, Zolotran Group acquired Pharmaply, subject to approval. Once Wuthers told us what he was up to, we decided to acquire the company."

Helena intervened. "Why would Wuthers tell you, after you hired us to find that out?"

"Ah, Miss Vaughn, if that is your real name, since you are being so slow, let me explain. I simply decided to have Mr Wuthers picked up so I could ask him that myself."

"So *you* kidnapped him," I muttered.

He laughed at me. "I 'borrowed' Mr Wuthers for a few hours until he saw the benefits of working together."

His phone pinged and he read it. "And thank you, I see your colleagues have returned the floppy disks." He held up his phone. "Now all the evidence is back with us."

I felt sick. Even though the phone in my sock was traceable, it might take Marek and Cleo too long to reach us. I looked across at Helena, still so strong, and I admired how she could be like that. I understood that now was the moment to be strong too; I just wished I could persuade my stomach and legs to behave.

"I think it's fair to say, Miss Vaughn, that your services are no longer required, and sadly, I don't think we will need to pay you, either." Street didn't look sad; he looked very happy.

Payment was the least of our worries. I tried sneering to match his, but with a queasy tummy, I don't think it came out very well.

"So you're just going to become another cheapskate drug dealer?" I was trying anything to delay the inevitable.

He smiled wider, and again my stomach cramped. I sat down on an easy chair before my knees gave way. One of the guards made to make me stand, but Street waved him away. "You really are behind the curve, *Mr* Jones. So what do you think is going on here?"

I told him they were making amphetamines and shipping them north. He laughed.

"And just how do you make drugs under the noses of hundreds of people?"

That was the very question Helena had asked. I didn't have to wonder any more—he couldn't wait to tell us.

"Simple! We make fake drugs. Placebos."

"But the disks contain real drugs." I found that logic was providing a good substitute for backbone.

Street beamed with pleasure. "Let me explain. When I heard this from my good friend, Bill, I couldn't quite believe it either." He started to count on his fingers.

"Step 1: You tell your staff you are making placebos of common drugs for double-blind studies.

"Step 2: You tell them it's a big secret, because if the doctors or patients find out it's *us* making the placebos, it might affect the results of the study, so they must tell their friends and family that we are making *real* drugs. This creates a false, but reasonable reason for complete secrecy, for the good of all.

"Step 3: In order to further conceal what we are doing from our competitors, we tell the staff we are making small quantities of real drugs, such as amphetamines, so if anyone analyses the chimney plumes or the waste, they find the right traces. So, some of our highly trained chemists enjoy themselves playing at drug making, which they are very good at.

"Of course, except for research, these drugs aren't approved, so, Step 4: As soon as they are made, they are put in barrels for disposal, and taken for incineration."

I had followed so far. Helena was looking a bit downcast, but I was determined to draw things out as long as possible. The longer we kept him talking, the better chance we had. I didn't want to get shot and dumped in a barrel.

Street was carrying on, thoroughly enjoying his performance.

"Except there are two little deceptions. Firstly, the placebos aren't being used for studies. They are being sold to gangs up north, through a front company. The front company tells the Pharmaply board that they have the rights to ask us to make the placebos, and pays them very well, so the board doesn't ask too many questions. What they don't know is that the front company is owned by my friend Bill."

"I'm sure the gangs aren't going to be happy with fake drugs," Helena observed.

"On the contrary, they know they are fake. Much safer than the real thing. And of course their customers don't complain because they got them illegally in the first place."

I marvelled at the double-cross. Helena also appeared to have cheered up a bit. I was having a hard time keeping up with her emotions. Then I decided I was having a harder time keeping up with mine. I was reminded of the first time I met her, waiting for the bus, that rainy night, but this time I was determined not to dither. It was time for a plan, and if I wasn't good at plans, at least I was good at making boxes bigger, and Helena was standing in what amounted to a slightly curved box.

"And the second deception?" Helena was genuinely curious.

"Ah, this is genius," said Street. He had waved his hands about so much that he had lost count of his steps and, after staring at his fingers for a few seconds, had to improvise. "The next step is to take the barrels of amphetamine destined for destruction, and move them back into the pill-making line, marked as a special corn-starch and sugar blend. These real pills are then sold to the gangs as well. But only Bill knows about this step; it's his little bit on the side. Correction, it's *our* little bit on the side. He comes in at night to do the swap-over.

"Then we move lots of barrels around, mostly empty, to mask exactly what is going where. Little and often is the motto. Like I said, it's genius."

Street clearly considered himself a genius by proxy, and was so impressed by his own performance that he didn't notice I had brought my foot up as though to sit more comfortably. I now had the knife concealed in my palm. I knew I couldn't rush all four guards, but if I had read him right, then we weren't about to be shot.

As the lift doors pinged everyone looked over to see who was arriving. I took the opportunity, sprung up and rushed over to Helena, cupping one hand behind her neck and the other around her waist. "Oh Emma, Emma," I cried, "I just want you to know that whatever happens, I've loved working for you. No, wait, more than that. I *love* you."

"Oh how *sweet*," declared Zolotran's Chief Research Officer, "let them have their goodbyes." He waved aside the guards who were about to wrest us apart. And thus I had time to slice through one or two of the wraps of network cable, and leave the knife in Helena's hands.

"I feel quite faint," she declared loudly, and sank into her barrel, taking the knife out of view.

Mr Large and Mr Little lifted the second barrel, *my* barrel, out of the lift and bounced it on the floor in front of me. Street nodded his head to tell me to get into it. I stood on the chair, and clambered in. One of the guards bound my hands behind me with another cable, this time green. Wuthers held up a barrel lid, and the metal locking hoop. I wondered how long I would last with that amount of air.

"I'd say you've got fifteen minutes. An hour, tops." Street smirked, as though reading my mind. I knew Helena would be able to bore a hole through her barrel if her hands were free, and so she'd be able to breath, but I doubted she would be able to cut herself all the way out of the barrel in time to free me too.

"Thank you," I said as I sat down in my barrel, "thank you for a really great life." And I meant every word. Five nights and days of pure wonder. All Helena did was snort. She really wasn't good at being romantic.

As the metal loop clamped shut, my senses were deadened. I could still see, the thick blue plastic did not eliminate all the light, and I could still hear, but only very low frequency noises. To my relief, they moved us into the lift straight away.

The sooner we were dumped somewhere, the sooner Helena could start to make an air hole.

Only my breathing was loud, and I tried to still it, but with so many thoughts, it was difficult. I knew Marek would find us because of the tracker in my sock, but I knew the battery would last longer than I would, so I wondered what state he would find us in.

I tried hard to wiggle my hands out of the network cable, but it didn't stretch at all. I realised I may not have cut enough of Helena's bonds to allow her to free herself. This thought filled me with despair.

I recognised the sounds of a pallet truck as I was rolled into what I assumed was one of the trucks. We were en route for the waste incinerator, of that I was certain. I could hear other bumps around me—other barrels being loaded. I hoped I wasn't at the bottom of the pile, not that it could make much difference.

It was becoming quite hot, and I felt my mind wandering. The last thing I heard was the truck engine being cranked, and barrels moving as we hit a bump. I passed out.

25 – A Much Bigger Box

It is a sweet thing to wake up, and a much, much sweeter thing when one realises one was not expecting to wake up at all. To be able to gaze into the eyes of the person one loves on waking is sublime. In my case, it was into the eyes of my dear Helena and the incomparable Cleo.

I didn't know it was Cleo immediately, but I didn't care either. The memory of them staring down at me is something I will cherish for the rest of my life.

They said the nicest things too.

"I think he's waking up." That was Cleo.

"He's an idiot." That was not.

I blinked, the light was a little harsh, and I saw that it came from Cleo's phone. Looking around I saw we were still in the back of a truck that was moving. I was lying on the top of a single layer of barrels, looking at the roof. I began to recalculate how long this air in the truck would last, but then I could feel a slight breeze—it wasn't airtight. I sighed in relief.

"Relax," Helena instructed, "Cleo says Marek's driving." I smiled like a happy puppy at the girl I had gone to rescue, knowing I probably couldn't rescue her.

"We're going to stop at the services," Cleo said.

"But what about the 4x4 filled with the guards?" I tried to get up, alarmed.

Helena snorted. It really was the most beautiful sound. "Marek scheduled them to go to Cornwall, and then scheduled himself to drive this baby. Cleo managed to slip inside while they were loading, and she found me once the doors were shut."

Helena suddenly looked very serious—even fierce in the phone's stark light.

She bent over me and kissed me long and hard. I wished I was better able to return the favour, but I had a pounding headache.

"That's for coming to rescue me.

"And later, I intend to thank you for the knife. When I felt that, I thought we had a chance." She gave a single stifled sob—it took me right back to the bus shelter. I didn't know what to say. It was good to be alive, but that aside, I realised this case had still ended in failure for her.

"I'm sorry about Street," I said. "He's a real rat. And I realise we're not likely to be paid." By which I was trying to let her know that I understood that I might not be getting paid. Helena must have invested thousands in this operation, and irrespective of any help I had given, the net profit was now below zero.

But what I didn't say was that I was more worried in case they felt I couldn't join the family because of any financial issues.

All these thoughts became irrelevant as we felt the truck braking, and a couple of minutes later we rolled to a stop. The door was opened swiftly.

I sat up on one elbow and admired the blue sky. Such a nice blue compared to the barrel.

"Quick," Marek said, "Street and Wuthers have followed us." I looked around expecting them to appear. "No, we've got a minute, they're a bit behind. And Cat and Celestine are behind them, and making ground."

We jumped down, Marek giving me a hand, and then he closed and bolted the doors. I followed Helena, Cleo, and Marek behind some cars and looked around. We were stopped in the trucking area of a motorway services, well away from the shops, and hence mostly isolated. I tried to sit down, but decided this wouldn't help my head feel any better and I preferred to be able to run if I had to. From our vantage point, I saw the other truck already pulled up alongside ours.

"Who's driving that one?" I asked.

Marek grinned. "Just one of their drivers. I told the system to schedule a rest here, and so he's gone to get a cup of tea, no doubt pleased at the early stop." I shook my head. These days, people will do anything merely because a computer tells them to.

We ducked down as a red MX-3 came to an abrupt halt in front of the trucks. Two very unhappy men glared out of the windows. Street got out, his hand hidden by his coat. Wuthers was less discrete. "Guns," Helena whispered. Marek just nodded.

Street and Wuthers were looking at the trucks, a little mystified. I understood how puzzling the sudden loss of the guards must be, not to mention the unexpected halt at the services. They probably hadn't realised they no longer controlled the trucking schedule.

Their brief survey was interrupted as, with not much more than a whisper, the Bugatti drew up, Celestine driving and Cat riding shotgun. Cat didn't bother with discretion at all. She stood up in the car as it rolled to a halt and pointed a 9 mm Uzi directly at Street.

"Cavalry's here," she declared.

Wuthers dropped his pistol and waved his hands in the air. Marek rushed out from behind the cars, told Wuthers to put them down. Celestine threw him some handcuffs, and he cuffed the man.

Street looked around for a way out, but by this time Celestine was similarly armed. He carefully placed his pistol on the floor. Helena and I moved towards the Bugatti, Celestine threw a pair of cuffs to Helena who secured his wrists too.

I hoped that was it, but Street had one more ace to play.

"So, Miss Vaughn," he spat, "what you going to do? Call the police?"

We looked at each other.

"I don't think so." Street continued. "A quick look at the CCTV and they'll see you're packing guns. They aren't going to like that. Plus you've impersonated a government official. In fact, now that I think about it, I think I'll have to tell them that you're the one who forced us to make these drugs. Who are they going to believe? Two respectable businessmen, or a petty sneak thief and her gang. I bet there's a criminal record or two amongst your lot."

Celestine growled. It was a very primal sound. I felt a renewed helplessness. It sounded as though we were cornered. Without a case, without our pay, and about to have to let these two weasels just walk away.

Then I remembered the knife. Or more precisely, the two little boxes I had moved to the other side of the Bugatti to make way for the knife. "Let's load them up—" I pointed to the other lorry, and then went to retrieve the boxes. Helena paused only a moment before she nodded and gave Street a little push in the right direction.

Marek made short work of the lock and then moved the white containers of drugs from his truck to theirs. I helped lift the two men up into the back of the truck. Celestine wanted to pack them into barrels, but Helena wouldn't let her.

"Don't make a noise"—Celestine pointed to one of the barrels—"or else." Wuthers backed away over the cargo, while Street just glared at her.

"Might as well make yourselves comfortable," said Marek as he shut the door. I tied the Veyron's tracker boxes to the rear bumper, and reactivated them.

***

From our hiding place behind the cars, we waited until the driver walked out of the services. He gave a cheery wave to Marek who was pretending to be talking on his phone. As we watched, the truck set off, the antenna wire of the tracker fluttering in its wake.

"In about thirty minutes," Marek said as we rejoined him, "that driver is going to have a very interesting time."

The toot of a horn announced the arrival of a minibus.

Alex leapt out, with Robert following more sedately, looking a bit flushed. I smiled as I remembered that I had once thought Alex was a boy. She hurried over.

"Oh, thank goodness you're okay." She hugged Helena, and then me.

Robert took the situation in in a glance. He searched Street's convertible and returned bearing a semi-automatic and the cash box we had seen earlier. Helena opened it and beamed. "My phone!" Robert gave her a long squeeze, and then stood in front of me.

"Thank you," he said slowly, as he very formally shook my hand. "Thank you for rushing in." I was embarrassed. "I think that's twice you've saved Helena this week. Maybe three times." Helena gave him a glare but he just smiled that enigmatic smile of his and said "What? You want me to spell it out?"

Helena was spared by Marek.

"Come on," he said, "we should get going. When whoever is looking for the Veyron descends on that poor truck driver, he will probably send them back here."

"Just a minute." Helena stopped him as he moved to the minibus. She motioned to the back of the truck and Marek opened one of the doors.

She sighed, looking at barrel after barrel of cornflour placebos.

"What can we do with these? Street won't pay us once he's in prison, and he was right—we probably can't enforce our contract with him without answering a lot of difficult questions. So"—she bit her lip as she surveyed the cargo —"any ideas how we can make some money from a load of corn-starch?"

We looked at each other. No one volunteered anything.

I wasn't really into cornflour so I wasn't thinking too hard about it. Instead, I imagined how Street would explain being in a truck with a whole lot of contraband placebos, plus a barrel or two of amphetamines. The thought made me feel better, and I smiled.

The smile was misinterpreted by Alex, who suddenly looked at me hopefully. My happy feelings drooped. I was going to have to disappoint her. She saw my face, and hers fell too, but her eyes still burned hopefully. She made a rectangular outline with her fingers to remind me of our earlier conversation about thinking outside of the box.

And that's when I saw the box. I turned to the incredible girl beside me.

"Fair Helena"—I flourished my hand, euphoria emboldening me to melodrama—"ask not what you can do with a truckload of cornflour, but ask, what can you do—with a truck."

It took her only a moment to smile. Marek regarded the almost new rig with a gleam.

Cleo squealed, "I've never stolen a truck before," and she was bounding towards the passenger door.

It felt good to see the tables turning back in our favour. Helena gave Celestine a big hug, and I recalled how wonderful the raven-haired girl had looked, standing beside Cat in the Veyron, Uzi at her hip, like some modern-day Boadicea. I desperately wanted to celebrate—to ride with Helena in the Bugatti, but I knew the moment was Celestine's.

I offered to ride in the minibus, and Helena's smile of thanks melted my heart.

I watched as the Bugatti with its dark and blonde heads disappeared, Celestine's head resting on Helena's shoulder. At the last moment, the blonde became a redhead. I sighed, unsure as to how I felt.

Marek laid his hand on my shoulder. "Come on, ride with us instead."

I just nodded and followed him to the cab. He held out the keys. "Want to drive?"

I smiled at him, and then realised he was serious. "I can't. I mean, I don't know how."

He doffed his head and stood aside to let me in, and then clambered up behind me and settled behind the steering wheel. Cleo was already inside on the left of the bench seat. She stopped examining the cab facilities and gave me a long hug which only partially worked given the sitting position and height difference. She seemed genuinely glad to see me, and it lifted me a little. She settled back, her arm locked through mine, holding on as though I might run away.

Marek took out his phone and connected to the Kombi via SSH. A few minutes later he passed the phone to me.

"You should do the honours; it was your idea."

I pressed the Enter button to confirm, and the truck was deleted from the Pharmaply asset list. A few clicks later and the logistics tracker was disabled. Marek said he would replace it with one of our own later.

Cleo squeezed my arm. "A whole truck! Not bad for someone who isn't a team player."

I was both happy and sad to know that Helena had passed on this bit of gossip. It felt good to be wanted, but realising the enormity of everything that had happened was threatening to overwhelm me.

Marek looked over and caught my eye as he started the engine. He nodded in sympathy, but said nothing. We slipped out the back route of the services and started for home.

Home. I already thought of the large house in the valley as 'home' and yet I realised there were a lot of assumptions in that idea.

I knew in order to stay, I had to be accepted by the group. Unanimously, Helena had said.

I thought on balance I had done a good job, and when it came to work, I had never lacked confidence. However, I saw I might be a threat to some in the group—to Marek, whose lover was currently wrapped around my arm; to Celestine, who was so fiercely protective of those around her. And I couldn't be sure about the others. Helena liked me, I was sure of that, but she had been prepared to break the group rules in order to let me stay. I knew enough of office politics to know that such favouritism could easily create division within this close-knit group. Such a division would not favour me, as the newcomer. No, a clear vote was far from certain.

But then I started to realise that my greatest enemy lay not in the group, but within myself. Yes, it had been an adventure, there was no doubt about that, and my life had changed irrevocably. I had relished the challenge and loved meeting these new people, but could I sustain it?

It was one thing to put on one's best face for a new crowd. One thing to show a bit of brilliance in one's work. But quite another to maintain a relationship. And I wasn't even thinking about personal relationships, I was just thinking about work colleagues—my sole experience. I knew too well how quickly I was unable to fathom what was expected of me, how quickly brilliance was seen as arrogance, and tolerance became exasperation. Everyone wears a mask.

I paused in my thoughts to give Mr Logical time to reply. I had half-expected him to make the 'mask' statement, but sometimes we prompt each other. However, it was Marek who broke the silence.

"Enjoying being the blue-eyed boy?" He was smiling, joking, I think, but it struck me at the very core. My own mask must be slipping. He raised his chin and eyebrows in question as he recognised my anguish, and then he turned back to concentrate on the road.

Cleo snuggled in on my left, both comforting and disturbing at the same time. I wanted to escape, but I knew it would be hurtful to shake her off. The rising surge of panic and proximity was about to explode when Marek started speaking again. His voice was low, and I had to lean over a bit to hear him.

"Ever been fired?"

I stared at him, wondering if it was meant as an insult. Mr Logical was listening intently, waiting to see what I would say. I realised this was the final nail in the coffin. I couldn't lie to these people to make them like me, but once they knew the liability that I was, they would run a mile.

"Yes." I hung my head.

"More than once?" Wow, talk about rubbing it in.

I took a deep breath and just nodded.

Marek paused and then caught me unawares.

"If an alien ship landed in front of us now and said they'd come to take you home, would your first thought be, 'What took you so long?'"

I stared at him as he peeled open my innermost being. I hadn't expected this. I wondered if it was a trick question—personally I wouldn't have thought of questioning aliens. After a moment, I bluffed, "Well, I'd be interested in their tech, of course." He smiled, dismissing the frivolity.

"And when you think of people en masse, do you say 'People do this or that', or do you say 'Humans do it'?" Until then I hadn't really noticed, but suddenly I saw how true it was.

I recalled a youth leader from my school days. "I remember once being asked what I thought was most important to me, and I said, 'being human' and he had laughed and said 'duh, of course.'"

Marek nodded, recognising my need. He stared ahead for a while and then spoke again.

"James, the thing is this: it's not easy being different. Most people are social animals—it's second nature to them, first nature even. Being social is what allowed us to survive in those earliest eras of human existence. Without working together, we would have perished as a species. Without cooperation, civilisation could not have been built." I nodded; I understood this.

Marek paused, and then came from yet another angle.

"Robert introduced me to Helena." I was surprised; I told him that Robert hadn't mentioned it.

"The consummate attorney," he said dryly. Beside me, Cleo giggled, her breath tickling my ear.

I felt better now about her being close. I wondered why I had difficulty with closeness. I looked at Marek, waiting for him.

"There were ... some issues." He trailed off. The three-quarter-sized human beside me stirred. 'Person,' Mr Logical reminded me. I thought we were both wrong, and found myself examining her ears again for signs of pointedness. She caught me looking and I wondered if she guessed.

By way of answer, she unlinked her arm from me, undid her seatbelt and rose, turning until she sat astride me. Giving me the tiniest peck on the lips, she continued her journey across me and sat between Marek and me. Cleo kissed Marek on the cheek, and then linked arms with both of us. He made her change gear while he ruffled her hair. She pretended to object but cuddled him closer, pulling me over a bit in the process.

Marek looked uncertain. I suppose he had something difficult to say, but didn't want to be rude.

"The point is, James, that being different can mean trouble." I knew this too well. "Not fitting in; not being good at social stuff; always being at odds with people; feeling alien—all these things can make you think that you're a liability." His use of my own word surprised me, but I was glad he was coming to my defence. Except he didn't.

"And you are." I tried to look hurt, but Cleo was looking at me intently. It made me want to look nonchalant. She laughed as conflicting emotions contorted my face.

"I didn't join the family at the first vote," Marek continued.

"They rejected you?" I was indignant. I couldn't believe that they hadn't seen his obvious, but perhaps quiet competence.

He smiled as he remembered. “There was concern, but it wasn’t them, it was me. I didn’t want to belong.”

I was stricken. ‘Not everyone wears a mask,’ Mr Logical finally responded. It was true. I had seen nothing but openness and transparency since I had arrived at the house. Any masks were strictly for work. I felt naked as Marek described my own conflict.

“Belonging has a price tag. It means giving up something of yourself. I didn’t want to give up being me, so I said no at my vote.”

“But you are a member now.”

“Luckily Helena believes in second chances.”

I thought of the girl I had met with the wet hair. The girl who had been willing to give me a first chance. The girl who was currently driving ahead somewhere with someone else.

Marek was speaking again. “Belonging means giving up enough self to allow the group to function. It isn’t easy, and it isn’t for everyone, but”—and here his voice grew stronger with conviction—“what you need to understand is that being different isn’t wrong. Humans have spent so long perfecting cooperation that it’s become normal. Normal is okay, but by definition it just means average. The problem is that not being normal is seen as a disability, instead of a different ability.”

I wondered aloud how this had escaped me my entire life. Marek just smiled and pointed out that it hadn’t.

“Everyone thinks of themselves as ‘normal’. What you’ve experienced is other people’s reactions to you. It’s made you think like you don’t belong on this planet, but the reality is, you just have other skills. And it’s those skills a group like this needs. Other people’s liabilities are our greatest asset. But”—and here he paused to make sure I was listening —“being in a group requires letting go of you; making a commitment to belonging. You’re good at rules, right?”

I nodded.

“So, being ‘normal’ enough to fit in can be learned. But you have to want to fit in, and that’s about heart and not about rules.” I nodded again. He had entirely expressed the turmoil within me. The allure of Helena, the promise of a home, but the dynamics of cooperation. Not being able to do what I wanted when I wanted.

The fear that had been generated by being fired from almost every job I had ever had. I had a very low expectation of social success. There were dangers of belonging, namely, that one could become un-belonged. It wasn’t better to have loved and lost—the loss was too great—it was better not to belong in the first place.

I saw the truth clearly. So closely had I been analysing the possibilities of not being accepted by the group that I had completely failed to see the problem I had of accepting myself.

I realised that all good things must come to an end. I gently detached myself from Cleo and moved away, staring out the window. She and Marek chatted quietly, but I remained silent the rest of the way home.

26 – Friends and Lovers

Marek slowly eased our prize up the avenue to avoid damaging the bodywork or the trees. He parked up behind the house, out of sight of the road.

Somewhat dolefully, I went to help Alex clean the hot tub, while Marek, Cat, and Cleo went to retrieve the Golf and the Kombi.

By late afternoon, everyone was back. Cat and Cleo went to work in the kitchen. They wouldn't tell me what they were making. I was sent to get some milk. It seemed like an excuse to get me out of the way.

By the time the sun was setting, Alex said everything was ready.

Helena told me to make myself scarce for thirty minutes. With some relief I took myself off and then decided to take a shower to try to get rid of the plastic smell that still lingered from the barrel.

I knew they would be voting on me joining the family. Part of me wanted them to say yes, but part of me was ready for the rejection, maybe even hoping they would say 'no'. I sat on the floor beneath the shower and felt the weight of the world descend.

Marek had been right, belonging had a cost. And that cost was the loss of self. Not the complete annihilation of my being, but putting myself aside in order to let others live alongside me. But who would lose themself like that? That was the question I could not quite find the answer for, and I knew that I lacked the internal structures capable of answering such a problem—it was too open ended; too ... social; and this led me to despair that crushed me, like giant talons in my back.

The water flowed, heavy, continuous, but wanting nothing. It was just there, its warmth and rhythm soothing me.

And then Mr Logical did something amazing. For once he

offered a practical solution that I didn't realise I already knew. He simply said, 'Protocol.'

In my mind, two computers faced each other. One extended a hand of welcome to the other, which, after a moment, responded. A handshake. A protocol exchange.

Computers do this all the time: one starts the conversation, another responds according to a protocol. The terminal letter of many network acronyms is P: HTTP, SMTP, FTP, and the P stands for Protocol—the language that allows potentially complex problems to be reduced to a simpler formality.

But there is a deeper beauty than the formal courtesy. There is a necessary symmetry in protocol. Every initiator must also be a responder. To know the 'receive' protocol, you also have to know the 'transmit' protocol. In order to work, both sides have to understand the common language—the protocol—the giving and the getting. Everything is mirrored.

You have to give to get.

And then I saw the symmetry of my problem. How, by letting go of myself, I allowed others to gain, and how their corresponding loss of self allowed me in—the symbiosis of belonging.

The water on my head started to clear my mind as though I was waking. I saw what I had missed previously. It was trust. Her trust that I would not dismiss the gift that she was offering so simply, so freely. Trust that I would not spurn the unadorned truth. The dawning realisation that all I had to lose was loss itself, and I understood this loss for what it was, isolation. I had found myself—or she had found me. Or rather, we had found each other.

I saw loss for the deceiver it was—so skilful, I had not even understood how in its thrall I was. But I was lost no more.

I was found. Founded. Rooted. Bounded. Bonded. Bound.

It was the simple truth of relationship—like the meeting of two craft in space. It wasn't enough to meet. For relationship, there had to be bonds. That overwhelming crush I felt was not talons; it was the grip of a thousand docking clamps latching progressively down my back, each one singing to my soul: 'Home; this is Home. You are Home'.

I let go of loss, and decided to allow myself to be found. I would trust them to allow me in, and I would trust myself to belong. I resolutely shut off the shower and started towelling myself off.

Okay, James, let's see how they voted, and I marched forward to find out my fate.

***

I walked out in my shorts, wearing a light blue T-shirt, feeling a little self-conscious.

As I rounded the rhododendron bushes that sheltered the hot tub, I noticed how each was now covered in purple or magenta flowers. I wondered how I had not been able to see such abundance before. Perhaps it was I that had shifted.

"Welcome, James," said Alex. She was in the water, half-turned, waving to me.

I stopped.

I saw I had been wrong. They hadn't wanted time to vote, they had wanted time to decorate.

Long garden candles formed an arc around the tub, their yellow flames tall and guttering in the twilight. Hung above the tub was a freshly printed banner. It carried the same simple words, 'Welcome James'. A cartoon truck adorned the left-hand side, a pair of furry dice the other.

Just below the surface of the water was a rim of LED lights, backlighting the bodies within.

I felt euphoric, not so much because I was happy—I was—but rather because it was as though I could see my future ahead of me, and it looked good.

For a moment I had a view of tomorrow, and all the days after that, stretching out like a road of promise; arising from where I stood and stretching up and over the house, winding lazily into the infinity of the saffron-fired sky.

I glimpsed forward in time, to freedom and belonging and meaning all at once. It felt simultaneously good but disturbing, and I realised that for the first time I really cared about the future, and I realised I had something to lose. The dread of loss counterbalanced my joy.

My eyes turned back from the sunset and I looked again at the banner, the candles, the balloons festooned on strings around the tub. I decided to make the best of it, come what may.

I climbed down the steps into the water, and then saw that I might be too formally dressed for the occasion. I wondered where it would be right to position myself.

Helena was sitting on the far side from the entrance—I wanted to sit with her—but she was flanked by Celestine on one side, and the twins on the other. I didn't think I could ask any of them to budge up.

The twins were making room for me between them, while simultaneously trying to change places with each other so as to be next to Helena. I paused in the waist-deep water and smiled at them, then at Helena, then at Celestine.

Celestine was positively glowing, and as I smiled, she inched over ever so slightly to her left, leaving a little gap between her and Helena.

I inclined my head to thank her for the courtesy, and sat between them. The twins made faces and wailed theatrically.

I glanced at Alex, sitting between Marek and Robert. She dimpled as I found her toes across the spa, and we played footsie ever so delicately, each pretending we didn't know it was happening. Robert was wearing a fedora and smoking a cigar. I wondered why no one was drinking.

Helena began, very formally. "Notwithstanding the banner, the vote has to be taken while you are here, James, and it has to be unanimous."

I gulped internally. Watching the vote was worse than just

getting the result. I had been doing the maths; unanimous might be tricky. I was pretty sure about most of them, except Robert and Celestine.

Robert was difficult to read, but Celestine was the real issue. It was one thing to ask her to make a space for me to sit—quite another to ask her to make a place for me to live—a place that would inevitably encroach on her own domain. Still, any space at all was a start.

Helena's tone became more serious. "Everyone, we have previously approved James on probation. Now it is time to vote on whether he should join the family. We vote first, then this time, he must vote too. I start."

I expected the long-drawn-out silence that seems to precede the revelation of any TV decision, and so I almost missed the word.

"Yes." She said it quickly and plainly, and squeezed my thigh under the water, then looked to her right. "Cleo?"

The twins replied in unison. "Yes."

This caused some confusion, so Helena just tried "Cat?" and got another dual yes.

"Robert?"

"Yes." He smiled openly as he replied, then returned the cigar to his lips and doffed his hat. I nodded back.

"Alex?"

"Yes."

"Marek?"

"Yes."

That just left one, the tough one.

"Celestine?"

I looked to my left. I remembered her reluctance before. I knew almost nothing of her, and yet she was looking right at me as though she could see my entire life. I thought the intensity of her gaze would shatter me, and then I saw what I had missed until now. She too was frightened. Not of me, but of the future.

In that moment I realised that no matter which way it went, I was already changed forever. Yes, I wanted more, I wanted to be *here*. But I also felt I could face tomorrow, no matter what or where. And as the fear left me, I relaxed my shoulders and smiled at her, loving her fierce loyalty and protective strength.

She looked down, exhaled, then looked up and into my eyes. I burned under her scrutiny, and then her face indicated she had chosen the braver path, and her hand found mine. She squeezed hard as she took a deep breath, her eyes warning me that she had better be making the right choice.

And finally she answered, clearly and firmly, "Yes, with all my heart." I loved her then, and kissed her on the cheek. Her eyes were damp; mine were too.

Helena addressed me and I turned back to her. I was still holding Celestine's hand.

"James, being of one mind we would like to ask you to join our family. To follow our rules. To remain faithful to us. To be kind and to be generous. To live and to work for us and with us. To love and to be loved.

"So now, tell us your answer, will you do this?"

I looked back at Celestine. I had seen her torment. I wondered what her story was, but irrespective of the past, I saw her now at peace, among friends. More than anything I wanted this. I breathed in and echoed her reply. "Yes, with all my heart."

Robert waved his cigar, and one of the twins jumped out of the pool to pour champagne. Celestine whispered in my ear, "That's Cat." Ah, I thought, now I shall have to remember my left from my right. Glasses were passed around carefully so not too many of the amber bubbles were spilt.

Helena made the toast. "To Home; Friends, Lovers, and Work if we have to."

We all raised our flutes, each picking a part of the motto they liked. I just leaned into her, raised my glass to the ensemble, and said, "Thank you."

Marek switched on the air, and we had bubbles around us too. I felt very buoyant indeed.

***

Forty minutes later the champagne bottles were empty and the snacks all finished. I was feeling pleasantly soporific and thinking I had had enough bubbles for a while. I wondered what was next.

The twins stood up, in front of me. It was an invitation. "You get to choose," Cleo said.

Celestine took my hand, but I slipped off the seat and further down into the water and rolled across her legs until I was able to sit on her other side.

I passed her hand to Helena, who moved a little closer to receive her. Celestine was looking right at Helena—I could imagine the fire in her face, reflected in the tenderness of Helena's eyes.

Helena leant over, but as they kissed, Celestine too rolled and manoeuvred herself away so as to leave Helena beside me again, a small gap between us.

Neither of us moved into the obvious space.

The twins made impatient noises.

I looked at them, so uncomplicated and straightforward. And then across at Alex, so earthy and serene. Marek was smiling, while Robert had moved round a bit and was talking softly to Celestine, his arm around her shoulders, offering her a puff of his cigar.

I looked back at Helena, so open; so complex; so sure; so vulnerable; so un-understandable. She had one eyebrow raised. I held her look, basking in the perfection of the moment.

And then, casually—to prolong things—and to tease her, because I wanted her, I said slowly, "Helena Fey, I hear blondes ... have more fun."

I glanced at the twins, who perked up at this exclamation.

Helena turned away gracefully and put her empty glass down on the edge of the tub. Then she stood, closing the gap between us, shooing the twins away with her right hand, staking her claim.

"Blondes," she said, sinking down into the water in front of me, "may have more fun."

She rolled her neck as though preparing to wrestle.

"But—" she leant in, her hand reaching behind my head as our lips met.

"Redheads. Kiss. Better."

And there was really no arguing with that.

THE END

www.ingramcontent.com/pod-product-compliance
Lightning Source LLC
Chambersburg PA
CBHW030412310726
48979CB00002B/379

* 9 7 8 1 9 9 9 7 1 0 2 2 4 *